That's My Baby!

Natalie threw a teddy bear to the front of the Jeep from her car seat.

"Don't get rough with me, girl," Kent said with a growl.

"Uf?"

"Listen, Gnat Nat. I know your sister doesn't hate kids. Confirmed it today. Called the director at that shelter in Pasadena. The woman thinks Caroline invented fantastic and 'couldn't be sweeter with little ones.' There's hope for you yet, kiddo."

He pulled in to Caroline's driveway. He twisted around to where Natalie occupied the car seat. She'd gotten rid of the cute dotted bow that women always cooed over. And he regretted offering her a chocolate cookie to keep her occupied.

It now decorated her hair. Her face, too. And her seersucker romper. She shot him a toothy grin, now darkened by a slash of melted black crumbs.

After he'd wiped up the worst of the chocolate with a handkerchief, he took a comb from his pocket to do something with her tufts of curls.

"Gnat Nat, it's show time."

Dear Reader,

April is the time for the little things…a time for nature to nurture new growth, a time for spring to begin to show its glory.

So, it's perfect timing to have a THAT'S MY BABY! title this month. *What To Do About Baby* by award-winning author Martha Hix is a tender, humorous tale about a heroine who discovers love in the most surprising ways. After her estranged mother's death, the last thing Caroline Grant expected to inherit was an eighteen-month-old sister…or to fall in love with the handsome stranger who delivered the surprise bundle!

And more springtime fun is in store for our readers as Sherryl Woods's wonderful series THE BRIDAL PATH continues with the delightful *Danielle's Daddy Factor*. Next up, Pamela Toth's BUCKLES & BRONCOS series brings you back to the world of the beloved Buchanan brothers when their long-lost sister, Kirby, is found—and is about to discover romance in *Buchanan's Return*.

What is spring without a wedding? *Stop the Wedding!* by Trisha Alexander is sure to win your heart! And don't miss Janis Reams Hudson's captivating story of reunited lovers in *The Mother of His Son*. And a surefire keeper is coming your way in *A Stranger to Love* by Patricia McLinn. This tender story promises to melt your heart!

I hope you enjoy each and every story this month!

Sincerely,

Tara Gavin,
Senior Editor

Please address questions and book requests to:
Silhouette Reader Service
U.S.: 3010 Walden Ave., P.O. Box 1325, Buffalo, NY 14269
Canadian: P.O. Box 609, Fort Erie, Ont. L2A 5X3

MARTHA HIX

WHAT TO DO ABOUT BABY

SPECIAL EDITION®

Published by Silhouette Books
America's Publisher of Contemporary Romance

to
William and Natalie
for being fabulous babies
and to
Gail Goyette
for always being the "sis" with an answer

 SILHOUETTE BOOKS

ISBN 0-373-24093-7

WHAT TO DO ABOUT BABY

Copyright © 1997 by Martha Hix

This edition published by arrangement with Harlequin Books S.A.

Printed in U.S.A.

Books by Martha Hix

Silhouette Special Edition

Every Moment Counts #344
What To Do About Baby #1093

Silhouette Romance

Texas Tycoon #779

MARTHA HIX

Award-winning author Martha Hix has never minced words. One night she crossed a crowded room to a hunk with the tall, dark and handsome prerequisites, and said, "I'm going to marry you." And she did. She and her husband are still happily married, and grandparents. When not writing contemporary or historical romance novels that are humorous, bawdy and fun, Martha delights in family and friends. A sixth-generation Texan, she lives in her home state and has been told she writes about "larger-than-life people, places so beautiful they break your heart, with a sense that anything is possible, if you're willing to work hard enough to make it happen."

Dear Reader,

Babies? Bah, humbug. Having gotten into the baby game at seventeen, I've spent my entire adulthood being a mommy. To this day, I turn when a child yells, "Mom!" I read—and wrote—to avoid kids. Then I became a grandmother. Wonder upon wonder, I got a new attitude. Babies are good. Babies are great! Who says you can't teach an old d— Um, who says that wine doesn't age well?

When I began *What To Do About Baby*, my own granddaughter was the same age as Natalie in the book. It's no coincidence that they are both named Natalie. I loved writing every page, since I had reminders of Gnat Nat…and her baby brother. It was easy to write Caroline's conversion—I had myself as guide.

How did my heroine, Caroline, become a mom? She and Gnat Nat are sisters, Gnat Nat born to their over-fifty mother through an egg donor. Hmm…women becoming mothers in their fine-wine years? Now, that is something I have no interest in exploring personally, but I do think the issue is intriguing. How about you?

It's a thrill and honor to be part of the THAT'S MY BABY! promotion. May you enjoy "my" baby!

Always,

Martha Hix

Chapter One

Caroline Grant had hit the bottom. Literally. This was no mere bad-hair day.

She lay in a heap on her living room floor, spitting dirt. Pain, fire-hot, inside the cast on her right leg, her shoulder angled atop a fallen crutch, Caroline gave in to a pity party. "Great. Just great. What else can go wrong?"

This was her second fall in three weeks, the first having tumbled her onto the San Antonio River Walk, but she'd had EMS to pick her up last time. Home alone had a whole new meaning.

Her tortoiseshell cat, tired of being ignored, sick of excuses, stuck her nose in Caroline's face. Her meow had the distinct sound of "Now!"

"Cut me some slack. I know you're hungry. So am I. No. I hurt too much to eat."

The mottled shorthair journeyed to the adjacent

kitchen, passing scattered Dominick's All The Way pizza cartons and a table that held a computer named Mr. Ugly. "Murr-ow. Murr-ow? Now!"

Caroline turned her eyes to the wheelchair that waited out of reach in her three-room duplex's shabbily furnished living area. She had to get aboard. Somehow. Somehow she had to reach the last can of cat food to Greezy's name.

The tortie returned to her fallen meal ticket. V-shaped head cocked, she twitched her tail. "Murr-ow."

A push rolled Caroline to her good shoulder; she tried to lever up on an elbow. Tried to. Luckily her leg stopped feeling as if someone drove nails into it.

Greezy waited expectantly. But not at all patiently.

"Sweetie, it wasn't a Snickers I was going after when I fell this time, you know."

Oh, for a Snickers!

Nothing would be accomplished, if Caroline didn't do something and now. She's spent thirty-one years helping herself. And others. Why should a second fall make any difference?

"I'll provide. I know you depend on me." She knew about greedy, needy females. Boy, did she ever.

Yanking the crutch from beneath a fiberglass leg cast, that went straight to the hip, she groaned. "I should have stayed in shape."

She shifted to her stomach. Renewed pain shot into assorted injuries, yet she inched to the wheelchair.

Once her behind was in the chair, Caroline straightened her cotton robe and vowed, "No more tries with crutches. Not for me. Crutches and I weren't made for each other."

She glanced to the kitchen. How could she reach

the top shelf from this vantage point? Being temporarily handicapped gave her a new appreciation for easy reach.

"Three more weeks. Then this cast is history. We'll live like queens. No more pizza for me. It's canned salmon for you. I may even grill it for you fresh."

As soon as she could drive, her second stop would be a bookstore for novels, magazines, the latest issue of *Enquiring Eye.* "For now, we're having a bad-hair life, aren't we?"

"Murr-ow."

That was when the doorbell rang.

Greezy ran behind the sofa; Caroline wheeled slowly toward the door. "Who is it?"

"Kent Mackay. From Dallas. I left a message on your recorder a couple weeks ago. I believe you spoke with my secretary when you returned the call. Ms. Grant, we must discuss an estate matter. As you know, I'm attorney for the late Don Perry and his wife, Ruth."

Ruth Perry. Caroline's recently deceased mother. Dead of some virulent disease, contacted while traveling. Dead along with her younger husband.

A mother unmourned.

"Go away, Mr. Mackay. I'm not up to company."

"This is important. Important enough to bring me in person from Dallas. Surely you'll allow a few minutes of your time."

If there was one thing good about this duplex, it had a window that gave a clear view to the front porch. Caroline wheeled to it and drew back the curtain a couple inches.

Her mother's advocate had a full gigabyte of sex appeal.

Tall. Lean but fit. Black hair. Nice profile, mustached. She'd never been one for facial hair, although his didn't look bad on him.

Above chinos and Top-Sider shoes, Kent Mackay wore an oxford-cloth shirt with sleeves rolled up to the elbows, giving a view of tanned forearms and a peppering of black hairs. He appeared around her age. She'd bet the last can of Tuna Surprise that he could hoist himself off a floor, hands tied behind his back.

The strange part was, he carried a diaper bag and a baby. Did he make a habit of taking his offspring on business trips?

Whatever the case, the kid could sell cute and never miss it. Ruffles, pink lace and a bow in light brown tufts of hair framed a rosy-cheeked darling. Not being an expert where babies were concerned, Caroline couldn't guess her age, yet the baby looked old enough to do a better job at walking than she could at the moment.

He knocked again. "Ms. Grant, open up."

She accepted the inevitable. The Hardwicke Law Firm couldn't be put off forever. Furthermore, she might be as cranky as an old cook, but she wasn't a total curmudgeon. It was hot outside, this being late July. The poor man and his little daughter could probably use a glass of cool water.

Opening a door? Another challenge. She angled the chair, unlatched the lock and back-wheeled. "Come in."

He did. After clearing the entry and closing it, the lawyer set the diaper bag down and turned to Caroline. He had the bluest eyes she'd ever seen.

They blinked, widened. "No wonder you didn't travel to Dallas for the funerals. And haven't been at your office. What happened? Are you injured, or is this something chronic?''

"I broke my tibia and cracked my knee, July fourth." A chuckle, despite general crankiness. "It better not be chronic."

The child whimpered, as if she were being held too tight. Kent loosened his grip, while sizing up Caroline and her situation. "Don't you have anyone to help you?"

"I don't need help."

He glanced at the coffee table that had first served as a telephone-wire spool and presently held dirty glasses and pizza cartons. "You're here alone, aren't you?"

"So what if I am?" New to town and her job, two weeks out of the hospital, she had no one to bring tea or sympathy, not that she'd ever ask for help.

"Didn't your doctor make arrangements for a visiting nurse, or something?"

"I belong to an HMO."

"That explains it." He stroked his daughter's pudgy arm.

Caroline found her mind wandering from aggravation. She took stock of Mackay the man.

He had the quality of confidence and education, and the blessing of handsomeness to round them out. Yet his black mustache added another dimension: the hint of a rogue.

"Do you know about Meals-on-Wheels?" he asked.

Meals-on-Wheels? He must think she was ninety-eight! "I've got meals on wheels. Dominick's Pizza."

"I passed a Chinese take-out. Sign says they deliver."

"Those guys think MSG is the first ingredient in recipes."

"I see your point. What about neighbors? Can't they help?"

The deadhead next door got evicted before she'd taken her big spill. Even if Mother Teresa were over there, Caroline wouldn't have begged rescue. It was the principle of the thing.

The baby took that moment to work a shirt button free and explore chest hair. The lawyer didn't seem to mind, until tiny fingers started yanking. "You little dickens," he murmured.

"Murr-ow."

The child pointed and tittered. "Kit cat."

Greezy twined around the stranger's leg to purr up at man and child. That hussy would do anything for a meal.

"Kit cat."

"Yes, Natalie. Kitty cat. Pretty kitty," Kent Mackay added generously, Greezy being less than comely, her coat an asymmetrical mixture of black, gray and dish water orange.

Nice guy, Caroline assessed. An oxymoron? Nice guy, Ruth's attorney? That mustache did tell a roguish tale.

He turned those bedroom-blue eyes. "Mind if we sit down?"

Yes, Caroline minded. But she needed to get the matter of Ruth over and done with. Forever. Which meant making her position clear to the attorney.

"I suspect you're thirsty," she said, remembering Texas hospitality. "Can't offer cola or iced tea, but water might be more quenching, anyhow."

"Let me. Keep your seat. I'll get the drinks."

This was where Ruth would have cooed and said something about nice men and gallantry. Caroline had a long memory. "This is my home, Mr. Mackay. I'll do the serving. Unlike my mother, I don't depend on anyone."

His eyes turned cool. "Two glasses of water will be fine."

Wheeling past him, she got a soupçon of testosterone-enhanced after-shave; it got to her, almost to the point of eliciting a grin. Yum. He did smell good.

Her hand shook as she went for glasses, not necessarily because clean ones were out of reach. After her big announcement about independence, it took eating the proverbial crow for her to say, "Well, gosh. Will you get the glasses, please?"

He had the decency not to gloat, a major relief. Striding into the kitchen to turn the tap, he held a cup to cherubic lips. His child swallowed, and he smiled. His was a great smile.

"That's a girl." He kept that dazzler on plump little Natalie. "That's a fine girl."

A small fist settled against his jaw, and her grin showed six little teeth. Such love, a father for his daughter. Caroline studied the hands in her lap. Once, she'd yearned for a child of her own. Best not to think about that.

"How old is Natalie?" she asked.

"Fourteen months. Walking and talking. Neither well."

The urge to hold the toddler came over Caroline. Not a good idea. She might drop her. Or was it motherly instincts, two years in abeyance, she feared?

Greezy, the tart, sashayed into the kitchen and made a figure eight around the attorney's ankles. Tail as straight as a dorsal fin, she next pranced to the cupboard. "Murr-ow?"

He scratched between Greezy's whiskers, a gesture drawing a purr. Yet he suddenly grabbed a handkerchief from his pocket to sneeze into the pristine folds.

"Mind if I feed your cat?" he asked upon recovery.

A lie slipped from Caroline's tongue. "She's not hungry."

His laugh filled the air, and it sounded way too good for comfort. He tucked the handkerchief away to say, "I know cats. Had two of my own. This one wants food."

"A typical man says his wife has cats." Caroline regretted the sour note, brought on by memories of Frank Grant, former husband. But how could she stop now? "Cats aren't the he-man thing."

The Dallas attorney wordlessly set Natalie on the cleanest part of the floor. He sneezed once more. Thereafter, he washed his hands, picked up a can opener and retrieved the last can of Tuna Surprise. His little girl giggled, thrust a diapered bottom in the air to get her balance. She toddled to the cat and empty bowl, plopping down to watch Greezy rear up and beg.

"Easy, Gnat Nat." His voice was tender but firm, anything but rascallike. "Be nice to the kitty."

She looked up at him, her hands clapping in delight, before turning that charmer smile on her reluctant hostess.

It was all Caroline could do not to offer a lap.

She gave her attention to Kent. As he forked Tuna Surprise into a saucer and bent to set it down, shoulder muscles strained his shirt. Caroline couldn't help being reminded of what she missed as a divorcée.

Natalie decided to lunge for the tortie, who, surprisingly, didn't unsheathe claws or have a fit.

A sweet baby cheek settled against whiskers. "Kit cat."

Greezy got a glassy look in her crossed eyes. The lawyer's daughter closed hers to hug the scrawny feline.

"What a beautiful child, Mr. Mackay."

"Knew you'd think so."

He crouched down to pull Natalie close. His trousers stretching across his groin served as a reminder of paradise lost—although Caroline hadn't known much paradise as a married woman. She averted her eyes. *Don't be a dirty old woman.* While not old, she did feel about ninety-eight at the moment.

Squinting upward, Kent said, "Let's back up to your remarks. First off, I don't have a wife."

A baby but no wife? Why not? Happened all the time.

"Secondly, all men aren't Frank Grant."

Her teeth snapped together. "How do you know about him?"

"Your mother kept up with you."

Then why did she never get in touch? An old and familiar ache twisted. Caroline never discussed Ruth. It hurt that, over and above rejection, she hadn't been accorded the same respect. But then, Ruth had never respected her daughter.

Kent, babe in arms, rinsed off the can opener and collapsed pizza cartons. "She knew you married Frank Grant, plumber and sports freak, a week after graduating from high school. You were barely seventeen. Lived in Pasadena, Texas. No children."

Caroline spent years trying for one.

"You did raise a stepdaughter," Kent added.

"Not really." Frank had forbidden the girl to visit more often than her mother demanded. Then she grew up. But she'd always loved Sheralinn. And always would.

"You worked at a Ship Channel petroleum refinery, turning valves. When you weren't at the refinery or keeping house, you volunteered at a shelter for under-privileged children. You even raised money for those kids, with spaghetti dinners and garage sales."

How had Ruth known?

Kent continued. "Eight years ago you defied your husband and enrolled in night school at the University of Houston. Graduated last May. Two years after giving Grant his walking papers. Fill-Er-Fast, a chain of gasoline outlets, hired you for the San Antonio district, in June. As a price analyst."

Her mouth dry, like the cotton that grew in the West Texas sun, Caroline asked, "How did Ruth find out?"

"Frank Grant told her. I followed up on it."

Frank had a mouth as big as the Lone Star State, except when it came to honesty with his wife. How he must have delighted in repaying her for leaving his hide to dry in front of the sports channel, in his re-cliner, with his favorite brand of brew.

Ruth and Frank—a pair best forgotten.

"Goody for them," Caroline said blithely. "You know all about me." Not all. No way could Kent Mackay know how much she despised her late mother. "I stake no claims against Ruth Perry's estate."

"Don't rush a decision, Ms. Grant. You may find it to your liking. And benefit. It was Ruth's last wish that you—"

Why listen to another word? "You have a beautiful daughter. I've enjoyed watching her. Now go."

"My daughter?" A face so confident before, now turned incredulous, as if he'd heard the world was flat. "Ms. Grant, didn't your mother speak to you about Natalie?"

"Why?" A portent crawled up her spine. Ridiculous. "Why on earth would that woman speak to me about this child? I have heard nothing, absolutely nothing, from her in years."

"We've got a problem." He began to talk fast. "It's dinnertime. I'll bet you're as hungry as we are. I hear Earl Apple's fries the best chicken in town. Why don't I drive over and pick up a bucket? You do like chicken, I trust."

She loved Earl's chicken. Her stomach hadn't been full since doing her nosedive and giving the tourists something to talk about. Hospital food—blah! These bare cupboards? She couldn't eat shelf paper, although it looked better and better, and more appealing than another Dominick's All The Way. Still, she wouldn't take chicken from a stranger, much less from Ruth's mouthpiece.

Especially not, since portent turned into rank suspicions of doom, settling into a sick feeling in Caroline's empty stomach. "What's the 'problem'?"

"Natalie is your sister."

Before Caroline Grant spun her chair around and wheeled toward the kitchen, ordering him out, Kent Mackay had seen surprise, then murder, in her tigress gold eyes. It had been a more than unpleasant shock, hearing about her little sister.

It had been a shock to Kent, too, realizing his clients had lied about contacting Ruth Perry's elder daughter.

The downside potential in this situation was vast.

What next? Leave? He tightened his arms around the orphan. This child deserved a home, with family.

She wouldn't be like him, thrown away as an infant.

That meant damage control. He lined up the positives. The Grant woman had it rough, rougher than she ought to. Add that to the investigator's report confirming verbal statements, Kent decided not to run.

He kissed Natalie's small fingers and glanced around the front room. It wasn't much. Papers littered the floor near a vintage computer.

The closest thing to decorations, outside the mountain of pizza leavings and dirty glasses, were an open check register with a string of entries to a pizza parlor, plus several letters from a health maintenance organization.

Natalie's trust fund, and the Perry home in Plano, could make life easier for both sisters. Caroline need never beg another job, as she had at the Fill-Er-Fast string of seedy gasoline stations.

He took two steps toward her. Fingertips pressed to her forehead, Caroline sat slumped just short of the kitchen. She didn't look like that devotee to liposuction, Ruth Perry. Ruth was one of those women Texas people called "fixie." Helmet hair never ruffled, never without a tube of lipstick or a wand of mascara.

There was an exotic look to Caroline Grant, and she had meat on her bones, which Kent admired. But she was a mess. That robe needed to see its way to the city dump. Her long golden hair, pulled back in a severe ponytail, emphasized an oval face of tawny complexion. A strained face that showed signs of beauty. She was the epitome of a wounded person.

She needed help.

He stepped closer. ''I didn't mean to give the impression I'd leave Natalie alone with you,'' he said, and Caroline boosted her chin. ''You can't be responsible for her. Not right now.''

''Get out.''

He settled Natalie on the sofa, then swung down to it himself. ''Why don't I check to see if Earl Apple's delivers?''

''They don't.'' On Caroline's face lay a thunderous cloud. ''Make tracks, Mackay.''

''I have a duty to my late clients and their daughter.''

''I don't. And I don't believe you, about Natalie. My father's been dead fifteen years. My mother died at fifty-nine. That child is not my sister.''

''Ruth became a mother at fifty-eight. Natalie is—was—her daughter. Ruth's last wish, and her husband's, was for you to take custody of their baby daughter.''

He could have sworn Caroline winked away tears as she said, ''Preposterous. And insulting.''

''You don't like children?''

''Why should I like this one? She's nothing to me. But it's not the kid I resent. It's Ruth. She always expected others to clean up after her.''

Funny-looking Greezy interrupted, inviting herself to Kent's lap. Another sneeze shook him. After graduating from the UT-Austin Law School and moving to Big D, he'd freed a couple of alley cats from the pound. It hadn't taken long to realize he and cats didn't mix. It broke his heart, giving those cats away.

Afterward, he'd visited an allergist, discovering he'd been a few antihistamines and electronic air cleaners away from keeping Tom and Hairy. He'd learned a lesson. Don't give up; there's a fix for most everything.

What would work with Caroline?

Short of his answer, Natalie's moon face screwed into a pout, the hunger-slaked cat now ignoring her. "Kit cat!"

Kent dug into the diaper bag, retrieved Natalie's "plug" and popped the pacifier into her mouth. She sucked, placated, and laid her head across his thigh. These past two weeks, while Natalie and her au pair stayed at his place in the Las Colinas area of the Dallas/Fort Worth Metroplex, had been great. He'd gotten pretty good at child care. It would be hard to give Natalie up. Much more difficult than giving up cats.

"Take that kid and get out of here," Caroline said again.

Kent pulled a blue-backed document from the diaper bag and leveled eyes on the Grant woman. Finger pointing at the door, she glared. Hunger and debility, he decided, did mean things to her.

Why wouldn't she allow him to feed her? Stubborn woman. As stubborn as Ruth had been vacillating.

Flicking the will open, he got down to business. "Don Perry, your mother's late husband, provided for their daughter. He and Ruth died within thirty-six hours of each other." After his abortive attempts to get Caroline Grant to Dallas, and before sending for the Perry remains, Kent went before Judge Brian Miller to gain temporary authority in all matters pertaining to the family. "There's a generous trust fund in place for Natalie's care, as well as for her future."

"How nice."

He ignored the sarcasm. "I'm executor of Natalie's trust fund. You were named in both Perry wills, as the person who'd take responsibility for her. Of course, your wardship isn't legal until you appear before the court. October fifteenth."

"Mr. Mackay—"

"Call me Kent. Mind if I call you Caroline?"

She looked like someone cornered by an insurance salesman, but Kent continued his spiel, nonetheless. "Natalie's au pair has given notice. Once Miss Gale returns to England, there'll be no one to take care of your sister."

"Too bad."

Yes, too bad.

"Kent...how did Ruth get this baby? Adoption?"

There was a softness to Caroline's voice, a mildness that spoke of decency. One could only hope! Hope? His investigator *had* augmented Ruth Perry's and Frank Grant's details by handing over a sterling report on a fine woman.

"Natalie was born to your mother," Kent said.

"She gave *birth?*" A laugh. A loud laugh. Loud enough to make Natalie spit out the pacifier.

Wincing, Caroline wheeled the chair closer. The cast rising above the hem of that god-awful robe had to be like a medieval contraption for torture. Kent had never broken a bone, but he wasn't insensitive to suffering.

"Did you call the folks at Ripley's?" she asked.

"The Perrys employed new-age methods. Don's the father, of course. But Ruth had a donor egg implanted."

"Donor egg? I've read about older women doing

that.'' Caroline yanked the band from her ponytail before raking fingers through hair that reached past her shoulders. ''Didn't that doctor check on Ruth's background before he played God?''

''Why should he do that? Ruth was a respectable married woman who wanted to have a baby with her husband. She couldn't. So the doctor helped them out.''

Bitterness ran rampant in Caroline's voice. ''He ought to be arrested.''

''You question the procedure's ethics?''

''I question my mother's ethics. Not every woman should have children. My mother was one of them.''

''Harsh words for a dead parent.''

''She was never a parent. Ruth abandoned me when I was nine. To 'find' herself. When Dad died, I was just short of seventeen. Alone. I was frightened, didn't know what to do or where to turn, and scared the authorities would find out I was by myself. I called my mother. She promised to take me in. I didn't see her until my high school graduation. She was between male saviors. Said she wanted a reconciliation. What she wanted was a loan. I handed over the insurance money my late father had left for my education. I never got a penny back. Or ever saw her again.''

Her admissions came as a surprise. Ruth had given a different version, one laying the blame of separation on George Danson, Caroline's father. Somehow Kent believed the daughter. Somehow? He was certain of it. Ruth Perry may have been his client, but he'd never liked the woman. She'd had a selfish streak that a blind man could see.

''Whatever the past dealt you, the fact remains this young lady—your sister—needs you.''

"What do you mean, needs me? I'm to rear her, or just look out for her interests?"

"She needs a home."

Caroline studied the baby who had fallen asleep in the middle of their discussion. Abruptly she swung to the side and knocked her leg against a redneck's first choice in coffee table. She swallowed a yelp.

Kent yanked Natalie to his shoulder, quit the sofa and took a giant step to help Caroline.

She wouldn't take it. "You and my mother expect me to take responsibility for a child I have no biological or emotional link to. I refuse."

"She's a great kid."

"That may be so. But I don't want her. I've got better things to do with my life than to rear my mother's folly."

"Why don't you sleep on it? I'll get with you tomorrow."

"No."

"She's a great kid," Kent repeated.

"I don't want her. Not now. Not tomorrow. Not ever. I won't have Ruth's baby getting in my way."

No wonder she was childless. If she'd had one, Kent thought uncharitably, she might have deserted it. Like he'd been abandoned at the maternity hospital. Left to exist in one rotten institution, or foster home, after another.

Natalie deserved better.

Better than Caroline Grant.

He reached for the diaper bag. "Fair enough. Goodbye."

With Natalie tucked to him, he made for the Cherokee parked in front of the Monte Vista duplex. Caroline might not look like her mother, but she acted like Ruth. No way would he let this child go to a bad home. Even if Big Sister begged.

Trouble was, conscience worked against anger. He'd sprung the news at a bad time, shouldn't have expected the moon. Add that to Caroline's past problems with Ruth. "I was too eager to win, Gnat Nat. To win at any price."

He'd allowed emotion to thwart strategy.

The mark of sorry lawyering.

What was the answer for the orphan in his arms? He mustn't quit. Caroline would feel better tomorrow. Tomorrow he'd use his head, and Natalie would come out the winner.

"Forget tomorrow. I'll wait till the day after. That'll give your sister time to get more desperate."

Kent Mackay, between now and then, would stock up on antihistamines. He'd need his wits for cajoling, charming and the art of subterfuge—the tricks of his trade and manly arts.

Caroline Grant *would* change her mind.

Chapter Two

"Who's there?"

"UPS, ma'am."

To Caroline Grant, he sounded more like that Mackay lawyer, now two nights in memory. "I'm not expecting a delivery."

"You know UPS—we run a tight ship. Gotta hurry. Apollo Health Maintenance Organization wants your signature."

What could the HMO have sent? Because of a mosh pit of trash bags blocking the window, Caroline unlatched the door. He wasn't a hunk in twill uniform. This was a hunk in jeans and a pullover shirt.

Black, coarse hair parted at the side, he looked quite tanned and fit, like the male models in infomercials that debility had forced her to watch. Well, he wasn't that bulbous. Kent Mackay was much too finespun for bulbous.

And, darn him, he lunged at opportunity.

"Liar." She crossed her arms over her breasts; he shoved a large box about the size of a moving crate into her living room, and slammed the door shut. "You're no delivery man."

"Wrong." His loafered toe tapped the box. "I'm delivering goods. Lunch. And other comestibles and supplies."

The scent of fried chicken wafted. Greezy sprang from a hiding place, yowling for the entrée, and Caroline herself might have ripped into the care package, if not for the source.

At least Kent hadn't brought Ruth's little daughter with him. Had he? "If you go out that door to fetch Natalie, I'm going to lock it behind you. For good."

When he hefted the box to the coffee table, she got a whiff of after-shave. Oh, the wonders of heady smells.

"Gnat Nat's at our hotel," he stated, "with her au pair."

"Good."

"Feeling better today?"

"Fine and dandy." Discounting her leg, the bruise on her shoulder, an empty stomach and slept-in clothes. Regardless that her boss at Fill-Er-Fast had called this morning—Filmore Wanek was antsy for his new employee to return to office. "I feel so great, I did housework."

Giving a profile view of his straight nose, Kent glanced at the still-untidy room, settling on the bags of trash she'd struggled to fill. "Quite an improvement," he overstated.

Smoothly he swung to the sofa and, knees spread, bent to the goods. Lifting the lid, he tossed a can of

Salmon Delight cat food into the air and caught it in the other hand. It had a pull-tab top that he yanked open. Greezy went wild.

"Stop that," Caroline ordered to no avail. "Shame on you! You ate twenty dollars' worth of anchovies yesterday."

"That's a lot of sardines."

"Not if you're ordering from Dominick's."

Kent gave a quick snort of laughter and set the can on the floor. Greezy chowed down.

He flourished disposable cutlery and plates. Next came food containers. And chicken—Earl Apple's chicken. A fist of hunger grabbed Caroline's middle. It hurt almost as much as a swollen knee or broken shin. Or the tendrils of conscience that nagged about leaving a child to twist in the wind.

But Natalie wasn't her problem. *If* she wanted to take in a stray kid, she could. Any kid but Ruth's kid. "If you think I'll compromise my stand for fried chicken, think again."

He heaped two plates high. Shoving white meat her way, he bit into a thigh and chewed slowly, thoughtfully. When a crumb dropped to his shirt, he took a napkin to be rid of it, and might as well have pointed to tanned skin and to the tight hairs crimping above his shirt placket.

"Don't concern yourself," he replied. "The matter'll be taken care of."

"If that's so, why are you here?"

"Masochism." He grinned. "I love catching hell from little old ladies in wheel chairs."

"I'm not little, nor old."

"You're older than I am." He balmed the sting by adding, "I don't care much for women my age—

which is thirty, in case you're wondering. I like a lady to have about a year on me.''

There was nothing attractive about an injured woman who couldn't even keep herself groomed. This shyster had something up his sleeve—Natalie—and he wasn't giving up. Caroline dared to ask, "How will the 'matter' of Natalie be 'taken care of'?"

"I'll call Child Protective Services."

"Child Protective Services?" It sounded very official, very austere. More serious than being left with one's ailing father. Almost as bad as being sixteen and watching him die. Certainly worse than facing the world alone at that same age. Hunger vanished. "Wh-what will they do with her?"

Kent finished off the thigh. "Probably place her in foster care until our day in probate court. Like I told you, it's scheduled for mid-October. She'll either stay in a foster home—or homes—permanently, or be placed in an orphanage."

He swallowed a forkful of potato salad. "This is great. Give it a try."

"W-wouldn't someone arrange an adoption?"

"Adoption is tricky." His face darkened with what Caroline took for courtroom dramatics. "Her future looks bleak."

Not wanting to be moved by tactics, she tried to harden her heart. The Perrys should have cleared the issue with their chosen successor before drawing up legal documents. "Why didn't you advise your clients to speak with me?"

"I did. They said you approved."

"They lied. You're not much of a lawyer. A good one would have followed up on their word."

"I had no reason to doubt my clients."

"You didn't know Ruth well." Caroline, despite her refusal to get involved, did feel sorry for the innocent child. "You talk lawyer-talk, yet you don't mention Natalie's wealth. That should make her a special case with your CPS people."

"If you don't take over, her money must be preserved till her majority. Nothing is set forth for necessities—the Perrys were adamant. They didn't want Don's money in strange hands."

"Those rats had an ulterior motive. They must've figured stipulations would work in Natalie's favor. Wrong."

Gazing at Caroline as if she were a rat, he let one silent moment lapse into another. "Does nothing get to you?"

"Nothing."

"Then it won't bother you, knowing...Natalie has a heart murmur."

His news hit in the softest part of Caroline's heart.

"Even if the courts approved an adoption," he added, his voice tight, "most adoptive parents shy from flawed kids."

"How...how bad is the murmur?"

"What's it to you?"

As Caroline knit her fingers and twisted them, her heart pounded. "Hospitals are awful. They must be horrendous for little kids too young to understand."

"Eat up, girl."

"When I...when I volunteered at the Pasadena shelter, there was a boy. With heart problems. After I went to college, I heard he had surgery. H-he didn't survive." She swallowed. "Will Natalie need an operation?"

"Does it matter?" Kent selected a second thigh.

"Stop toying with me. You know. Tell me."

But he said nothing.

A wealth of scenarios played in Caroline's mind, none pleasant. While he ate yet another thigh, she concluded: he wouldn't have mentioned the heart murmur if it wasn't bad.

Her voice displaying too much emotion, too much of herself, she asked, "She'll need surgery, won't she?"

The thigh in his hand didn't seem quite as appealing at the moment; it hung limply.

"Kent, she can't go through an operation alone. You'll see her through it, won't you?"

He smiled at Caroline, the expression as confidence inspiring as a doctor relaying a poor prognosis. "I shouldn't have troubled you."

Why, oh, why did Caroline get a sinking feeling? He counted on it, of course; she knew it. *I don't wanna care about that child.* Besides, it wasn't as if Natalie were used to constant attention from Mama. Mama couldn't have changed that much.

Yet Caroline asked, "Surely Natalie has someone. What about Don Perry's family?"

"Not another word until you've eaten." Kent eyed her housecoat-decked form. "If you're not careful, you'll dry up and blow away."

Shamefully relieved at no mentions of Natalie, Caroline retorted, "If this is where you say you like fat women, I'm not buying into it."

He angled far enough in her direction to slide the tips of his fingers across her good knee. His gaze took a languorous trek up to her eyes. "You're not fat."

Somehow she knew she ought to be insulted by his blatant lie. Somehow she wasn't. She marked it off as the tactics of a wily lawyer, and figured he'd probably taken some course in law school, something on the order of "When all else fails, flirt."

Kent eased against the sofa, lacing fingers across his flat stomach. "Greezy's about finished with her meal. If you don't eat this chicken, it's hers." He proceeded to place the untouched plate in Caroline's lap, giving her another whiff of what she assessed to be expensive sandalwood after-shave mixed with man, all man. "Eat. Now."

Her father used to say it was a sin to waste food. That excuse in mind, she ate. Wow, did it taste good! Chicken and fixings put her in a sensible frame of mind. She'd wiped many tears. Her stepdaughter's, as well as for the children at the shelter. What would be wrong with making a few trips to the hospital to give a sickly child someone to cry to?

Right then, purrs like a small motor in second gear reverberated through the room, Salmon Delight having mollified Greezy. The tortie licked her paw and pranced to the top of the TV, where she curled up to bask in herself.

Amazing, Caroline realized. Kent hadn't sneezed once.

"Watermelon," he said unexpectedly and patted the box. "After I put these groceries away and help you get tidied up. Watermelon in the backyard."

"No."

His gaze cruised over her pitiable form. "Yes."

"I can't negotiate the steps." A lame but true excuse.

"I'll help you."

"I'm heavy."

"You're not." He made an exaggeration of flexing arm muscles. "I'm strong."

After weeks in close quarters, she yearned for fresh air. She hadn't been outside since the Care Cab driver carried her from the hospital. That had been a frightening moment, knowing she'd enter this house and be on her own.

"Let me be your legs," this man offered.

She'd eaten his food, why not further impose? Because that was the sort of thing Ruth would do.

"You're a proud woman," he said, reading her mind. "I realize you don't like being dependent, but it's just watermelon. And I am strong. Let me prove it. It's good for the male ego."

"You've got an ulterior motive. Baby."

"Undoubtedly you weren't calling me 'baby.'" He got a wounded look in those incredible blue eyes. "My skills in the eligible-bachelor department must be lousy. I thought you could tell I'm interested in you."

"I—I'll bathe on my own. Watermelon sounds great."

"Let's get busy." He took a flexible shower attachment, plus two clean towels, from the box. "These'll come in handy. I'll install the hose, then we'll get you bathed and shampooed."

Her mouth dropped. He figured to *bathe* her? This near stranger? This mouthpiece for Ruth? "No way."

"Have you got a portable seat for the shower? Can you get a plastic bag over that cast? You need to let me help you."

"Over my dead body."

"I prefer you alive and breathing fire." He grinned

and settled his gaze on her chest. "I'm not into necrophilia."

"I'm not about to let anyone—especially you—bathe me!"

Shaking his head as if dealing with an alien from Planet Tough Nut To Crack, he said, "I'm trying to befriend you. You need a friend. Or a nurse. I'd say it's time you accept help."

In the past Caroline had forever presented a neat appearance. She'd lately tried to keep herself sponged clean, a real bath having been out of reach and beyond possibility. Three more weeks of this? But a *bath?*

Caroline wasn't overly modest, yet... "You're not seeing me naked. If—"

"If you're wearing panties and bra, leave 'em on."

"Since you've been ogling me like a Bangladeshi at a covered-dish supper, you know what I'm wearing."

One edge of his mustache lifted while he shrugged—an admission of guilt. "Will you allow me to help you get ready for the bath? You can keep the robe on, if you please."

"This is crazy. The nth degree of absurdity."

"Lean on me. I like damsels in distress."

"A knight in Yuppie armor, are you?" Caroline knew gallant specimen existed, although she hadn't seen one since her father died. Gallantry wasn't taught in law school, was it?

"Will you let me help you?" Kent repeated.

Comparing him favorably to the late George Danson, Caroline Danson Grant, independent woman without independent means, gave in. "If you'll help me into the shower—and back out, closing the door behind you—I will."

His face boosted into a smile of triumph.

Unfortunately, the smile vanished. It didn't take long to discover he was no handyman. He didn't know one end of a wrench from another. It took her instructions to get the shower nozzle off and the new fixture on, but Caroline found his ineptitude charming.

Those hands weren't made for mechanisms, but she'd bet anything they had their skills.

Furthermore, Kent Mackay did exactly as she wished. He readied her bathroom as she collected clean clothes. He gave solicitous attention while escorting her into the shower stall; he backed out graciously. The doorknob's sharp click gave witness to his keeping a distance.

Maybe he wasn't such a bad sort.

Caroline's opinion of Kent further elevated, once she was showered and had struggled into cutoff sweatpants and a short-sleeve blouse; he helped her back in the chair. He really was strong, since he lifted her as if she were a feather pillow.

He might be a good sort.

"That's a nasty bruise on your shoulder," he commented, concerned, as he wheeled her into the bedroom. "Looks fresh. You've fallen, haven't you?"

"I haven't gotten the hang of my crutches."

"Have you talked to the folks at the HMO?" Having rounded the chair, he bent at the knees to take her hands in his. "Do they know you're without adequate facilities?"

"No." Trying to disregard the hormones that sat up and danced in her system, she withdrew from his interesting touch.

"Shall I call the Apollo people?"

"Don't you dare! Fill-Er-Fast is self-insured. They pay my expenses. I won't take advantage."

Kent stretched to stand, giving a too-interesting view of his groin, one that almost caused her to miss his next words: "What good will you do them if you fall again, and it prolongs your convalescence? Your boss should've seen to your comforts."

Glad when Kent stepped back against her pasteboard dresser, she got a grip. "Filmore sent flowers when I was in the hospital."

"Call the damn HMO, Caroline."

Common sense agreed. Besides, she could make it up to Filmore Wanek in overtime and one hundred and ten percent of her efforts, once the cast was history. "I'll call tomorrow."

"Good girl. I mean, lady. Woman. Gal. Chick. What do you prefer I call you?"

"Chick?"

"A chick is too smart to be a babe, too hip to be anything but her own woman."

That didn't sound so bad.

Sincerity in his features and voice, he added, "I don't want to offend. I try to watch out for PS."

"Does PS have anything to do with PMS?"

He laughed, the sound rich. "PS—political sensitivities. It's a buzzword for politically correct."

"I am out of the loop. Guess I'm not PS at all, since labels don't bother me. Call me whatever you please, as long as it's not to wait on you. I'm a chick along those lines."

"Experience being the reason?"

"Marriage being the reason." She owed no explanations, but made them anyhow. "I'm jaded. I failed at marriage, but that's okay. I married a failure. Frank

Grant may have engaged in honorable trade, but he padded the bills at his plumbing shop to pay for tickets to sporting events. Which makes him a crook.'' A crook and a liar. He hadn't even been honest about himself to his *wife*. "I don't like people I can't trust."

"You can trust me. We may've started out on the wrong foot—pun intended—but I want you to judge me by my deeds, not by another man's faults."

Not a woman to mince words, she commented, "You seem to be a good egg. Perhaps a gentleman."

"Not a chance. I am just a man, after you and your body. A one-eighty from PS." He growled, eyeing the left leg exposed beneath the frays of snipped sweatpants. "You've worked up another hunger in me. I've always had an appetite for thighs."

A grin flipped the corners of her mouth. Her ex-husband had never been a flirt. His idea of mating had been a paw creeping under the covers to her breast and a "You ready?" It had taken much coaxing to fire Frank into giving her any sort of satisfaction. After her divorce, she didn't pay attention to men, her education being her first priority.

But it did feel good, being in company with a guy who looked as if he could start his own fires.

She teased, "You'd best have strong teeth. Or stick to fried chicken. This cast is made of fiberglass, you know."

"You won't be in a cast forever."

"But you'll be in Dallas," she pointed out.

"I've got good transportation. I like to drive."

"I believe we settled on watermelon."

"Watermelon, it is."

Watermelon was the last thing on Kent's mind.

God, I can't believe I told her to judge me by my deeds.

True to his calling, he didn't feel much guilt over his game of charming her into submission, nor for his exaggerations, even though he knew he ought to, as a *man*.

He turned an eye to Caroline, here in her bedroom. She looked better for her shower. And she did things to those cutoffs that ought to be outlawed. The one leg exposed had a nice shape to it, just plump enough. He didn't like boyish hips; she didn't have them. He appreciated her true hourglass figure.

But that beautiful mane of dark gold hair was wet and needed fixing. He'd never brushed a woman's hair in his life, but he suddenly had the urge for firsts.

He picked through the stuff atop her dresser, his fingers curling around on a hairbrush. A picture—a soldier in a Korean War uniform—caught his heed. "Let me guess. Your father."

"He's the only important person in my life."

Then she'd led a lonely life, something Kent could identify with.

He let go the subject, but positioned himself behind her. "Let's get your beautiful hair fixed."

Hairbrush teeth met her scalp. Gently he dragged bristles through thick tresses. He could get used to this.

"No man's ever brushed my hair," she admitted. "It sure beats the old paw-under-the... Well, never mind."

Kent got the message. That ex-husband of hers must not have been much in the technique department. A shame. Caroline tended to be as fractious as her cat, and too stubborn where Natalie was concerned, but Kent enjoyed doing for her.

It felt damned real, giving her his attentions. Never before had he felt the male instincts to provide and to protect a woman. He liked being leaned on. This was his first clue the game might be on him.

Kent Mackay was simply amazing.

He'd tended her, like a lady's maid. And he'd been tender, doing it. Caroline liked that.

Thereafter, he insisted on tidying the bath mess, and ended up doing more. He collected trash and washed dishes. He lined the counters with necessities, all within her reach. It felt weird, trailing in her wheelchair, watching someone do her work. Never in her life had anyone else done her chores.

Actually, it had a rather pleasant feel to it, the sort of thing she could get used to, if she wasn't careful.

"Finished," he announced. "Want a soft drink?"

She declined, but Greezy spoke up. "Murr-ow."

The cat helped herself to Kent's lap, once Kent sat down to drink a glass of cola. The man relaxed within Caroline's reach and filled her overstuffed living room chair to its best advantage.

"You haven't sneezed today," she said.

"Chick, I come prepared."

She laughed, feeling good for being clean and having an orderly house. "I do appreciate your kindnesses. A few weeks back, I never dreamed it could be so much trouble to be laid-up. I have a new appreciation for the challenges of the handicapped."

"What would you give for me to show up with a saw?"

"Wise guy. That's a cruel question. You know I'd do anything for a good saw."

His eyes glinted. "Anything?"

Sexual energy arced. But sanity surfaced. If she didn't quit the mating dance, he'd get the impression he could romance her into anything, including a change of heart on that baby.

"What sort of life do you lead, Kent?" she asked, to make neutral conversation. "Tell me about yourself."

"I work. My law practice consumes my time."

"Where do you tan?" she asked, her question awkward.

His eyes cruised down her form, his mustache twitching. A palm smoothed up her good thigh, eliciting the intended response. "I tan to the thong line."

Gulp. She would not challenge him to prove it. "I meant to say," she corrected, "if you're busy as all get-out, *when* do you have time to tan?"

"I tan easily. Which is good, since I don't bask in the sun. Matter of fact, I've taken but a single vacation in my life, and it was business connected."

"You must work out," she blurted.

"Not really. Blame it on my gene pool."

"Your father has a great physique?"

"I have no idea. My parents didn't see fit to rear me."

Caroline blinked. And read between the lines. He, like she—and Natalie, too—hadn't been afforded the best childhood.

Seeking to ease him, she said, "When I was a kid, I loved 'The Brady Bunch' and reruns of 'Father Knows Best.' I thought everyone else had happy homes. Crazy, wasn't I?"

A low rumble of laughter echoed. "Television gave me the idea all *Yankee* families were happy."

"I don't know what happened with your parents, Kent, but...I'm sorry for you."

"Hey, don't be. I'm fine." His tone said, "Drop it."

She did, but engaged her mouth before thinking. "You tan easily and don't work out. Next you'll say you're too busy for a love life." *Where is your head, making a come-on statement like this?* This guy played with her wits like no painkiller could.

"Are you offering?" he asked with deep resonance.

"I don't have a love life. By choice. I need to build my career," she said honestly. It was all she wanted.

She tried to convince herself about the latter. She'd done a lot of self-convincing since the breakup with Frank. It hadn't been easy, life. A neophyte analyst in a male-dominated field, she hadn't impressed the petroleum industry's Seven Sisters into giving her a chance, even though she had experience in the technical side of petroleum. It took groveling to impress Filmore Wanek. Now she must prove herself at the lower end of gas stations, with a cigar-chomping boss who wore white patent-leather shoes and told sexist jokes of the dirty variety.

"Tell me something," Kent implored. "Why didn't you include your ex-husband on the most-important-people list? You lived with the guy for a dozen years."

"Twelve years was long enough to remove Frank from any list that doesn't start with *S*." One night clenched it.

"Why did you stay around so long?"

Twelve frustrating years of marriage ended the night Frank owned up to a lie of omission. Even now, it hurt. "When hope springs eternal, it's a tough beast to slay."

Kent set his finished soda down and removed Greezy from his lap. The latter offended the tortie, who gave a series of sharp left hooks to his forearm. "Murr-ow!"

She stormed away, growling.

"How 'bout that watermelon?" he asked Caroline. "Let's do get a breath of fresh air."

Kent again made good on his brag about strength. He got woman and wheelchair down the porch steps as easily as he'd toted Natalie around. Just when she quit thinking about the rotten end of her marriage, she had another unpleasant thought: Natalie.

Small waif with a bum heart.

Another of Ruth's ill-conceived notions.

Someone else to pay the price of that woman's selfishness.

The watermelon no longer held appeal. As a blue jay hopped from a hawthorn limb to feast on a mountain-laurel seed, Caroline pushed her untouched fruit to the picnic table's center. A gentle breeze blew. The sun had never shone this brightly, yet she'd never felt more like a total bitch. That flawed tot, alone in this big world, needing surgery and a mother's love.

"What about Natalie?" she asked. "You never answered when I asked if Don Perry's family could step in."

"What if I told you Don's father is in the slammer?" Kent spoke tightly, in a voice roughened by disgust. "Convicted of stabbing a topless dancer to death?"

"What an awful person." A shiver of revulsion shook Caroline. "Surely Don's mother isn't as bad."

"What if I told you she runs a 'tanning' salon in

Montana? One of those places that caters to men. If you get my drift."

"Oh. One of those. No, I don't suppose Natalie has a future with them."

"Wait. Hold up. I'm putting you on. Don comes from unremarkable stock. His folks live up in Alaska. But they can't take Gnat Nat. Don's father is paralyzed. His mother's got her hands full with him. Don did set them up financially, but—"

"Kent Mackay, that was cruel of you, teasing me that way. But I'll forgive you—this once." Her mind more on Natalie than an offense to her sensibilities, she asked, "How did Don Perry get enough money together to provide for his parents and to leave an estate?"

"He won a huge settlement in a lawsuit."

"Ruth must have been thrilled."

"She was. I was there. As Don's attorney."

"Really?" Weren't attorneys who won big lawsuits in the money? "Young as you are, I figured you for a struggling lawyer, representing families in things like wills."

"I'm a litigation specialist."

"You can't be rich. You're too young to be rich."

"You're too young to be so cynical." Sunlight twinkled in his eyes. "I've done well for myself. I graduated early from school. I've been an attorney for eight years."

She admired his drive, his success, although it made her late start seem all the more paltry. "How did a litigation lawyer end up the executor of a little girl's trust fund?"

"I drew up the Perrys' wills and accepted executorship as a favor. I liked Don Perry. He was a fine fellow."

Caroline didn't have an opinion of her late stepfather, but she could see that Kent had respected him. "You're being a good friend, looking out for his daughter."

"I'm honor-bound to do it. And it's what I want."

In this day and age, when honor didn't have much value, Caroline respected his. "What about the egg donor?"

"She's a single mother with three kids to support."

"What about that trust fund you bragged on? Seems to me money would take the sting out of a fourth child."

"As I said, if you don't take Natalie, the money is frozen until she reaches eighteen. Even if that weren't the case, the donor made it clear she isn't interested in 'repercussions.' She's still not interested."

"But I'm supposed to be?"

"You have a void in your life," he said and stuck needles in one tender nerve. "Natalie could fill it."

"Wrong." Caroline scowled at a superior visage. "I've always had someone else's welfare to consider. My father's. Frank's. For once, I can live for *me*. I think I've earned my freedom."

"Sometimes, Caroline, plans have to change."

"Enough watermelon." Her line of sight moved pointedly to the duplex. Oh, to have the power to get indoors, unaided. "I'd appreciate your help up the steps."

"And I'd appreciate yours."

"I feel sorry for that child. But I won't take her."

"You won't want an update on her condition?" he asked.

"Oh, dammit, play fair!"

Sunlight gleamed on his dark head, highlighting the blue in black. Disgust dulled his eyes. "You disappoint me."

His reaction hurt Caroline more than it ought to. "Since Natalie means so much to you, why don't *you* rear her?"

"I can't."

"Work's that important?" she goaded.

"Something like that."

"Representing a middle-aged woman who wanted to hang on to her youth and steal the last of mine—such an important career."

"You're not pretty when you're being hateful."

"You'd be prettier without hair over your mouth. But I suppose you need it for twirling, when you do your lawyering."

Red crawled up his neck. He appeared on the verge of throttling her. "Could be I hide behind my whiskers. Like the real Caroline hides behind a nasty disposition."

Shamed, she said, "I don't claim to be Wonder Chick. I have too much anger to bend to my mother's will. But I do apologize for my remarks. Actually, I find you quite handsome."

"That's a start." He stepped in front of the wheelchair to hunker down on his heels. "But if you want back in the house, you've got to promise...you'll see Natalie one more time."

"Not until her surgery." Caroline slammed her big trap.

"Ah-ha! You aren't heartless." He smirked. "Gnat Nat's heart condition did get to you."

"Not true," Caroline lied. "But I, but I…well, I don't know what to say."

"Just say okay. To one dinner. Tonight."

"No way."

"Been nice knowin' you." He sprinted across the yard.

Stranded. No possibility of wheeling over the lawn. He had her. She knew it. He knew it. "All right! One dinner."

"Tonight?"

"Tomorrow night. Eight o'clock."

"Make it six. Gnat Nat goes to bed by nine." Kent rounded the wheelchair to give it a shove toward the duplex's rear porch. "Don't worry about a thing. I like to cook."

I think I'm the one who's just been cooked, Caroline thought morosely.

Chapter Three

"Gnat Nat, I strung your sister along about the heart murmur, but I had to." Kent looked for oncoming traffic as he drove to Caroline's house the next day. "She may've said one thing, but I saw compassion in her eyes."

Kent Mackay had read that elders should converse with youngsters to develop communicating skills, although he figured the experts didn't mean talk such as this. Which didn't stop him. "No Texas lawyer worth his salt would've missed it, the feeling in Caroline's eyes."

No response came from the Cherokee's rear seat.

Kent turned off McCullough Avenue. "I said those things to your sister for a reason. Some children don't stand a chance in the hands of state care. At least that was my experience."

Therefore, he'd used the bitter seasonings of his

own history to let Caroline think the worst about her sister.

True, Natalie's pediatrician detected a heart murmur during her second checkup, but a later report listed no such murmur. The doctor, nevertheless, advised follow-ups.

"I made an appointment for you," Kent said to Natalie. "It'll be weeks before Doc McBride can work you in."

"In?"

"I should set your sister straight." Warning signals flexed through his brain stem. "What if she uses it against us?"

The child in the car seat threw a teddy bear to the front of the four-wheeler, as if she objected to intrigue.

"Don't get rough with me, girl," he said with a growl.

"'Uf?"

"Don't mock me, either." Kent slowed the Jeep to let an elderly woman cross the street. "It's hard enough dealing with your sister."

The stumbling blocks to getting Natalie a permanent home were manyfold but, he believed, correctable. Kent hadn't lied about the Perrys' demands. But their attorney was no idiot. Despite his promise to Don, he could break their last wills and testaments, if need be.

"As for your sister..." An image now formed, conjuring a helpless woman strapped to a fiberglass cast. A lady in need of his strengths. A lovely woman who reminded him of his own needs.

Which were many.

"I went to her with forethought aplenty. Bingo. I did it." Charm had backfired, yet Kent got a distinctly male tickle in his briefs. "Can't say I don't like a challenge. But she was downright hateful, making that remark about my mustache.''

The mustache was a sore spot with Kent.

But Caroline couldn't have known that.

''I know she doesn't hate kids,'' he said. ''Confirmed it today. Called the director at that shelter in Pasadena. The woman thinks Caroline invented fantastic and 'couldn't be sweeter with little ones.' There's hope for you yet, kiddo.''

For a while there, he'd had his doubts. Strange, how things were turning out. He'd meant to make a quick trip to San Antonio, as a pseudostork, delivering a baby. This was his fourth day in the Alamo city. He decided not to stew over spending days away from his office.

By now he and Natalie had reached the duplex. It was small, built of stucco and surrounded by a privet hedge, flowering shrubbery and oak trees. The dwelling's heyday had probably been before Pearl Harbor, its last coat of paint in the Age of Aquarius.

He pulled into the driveway behind a compact car that a clerk in the motor vehicle department had registered to Caroline Grant, eight years previously. Kent turned off the engine, but he didn't jump out of his new Cherokee. Resting a wrist on the steering wheel, he sized up the duplex. What would happen tonight?

''Kit cat?'' floated from Natalie.

''Gnat Nat, it's showtime.''

He twisted around, to where Natalie occupied the middle of the back seat, safe and sound in the best place to transport a kiddo. He'd read up on child safety.

Natalie had gotten rid of the cute dotted bow that women always cooed over. He scowled. Above the bow's loss, he regretted offering a chocolate cookie to keep her occupied between the hotel and the Monte Vista section of town. It now decorated her hair. Her face, too. And her seersucker romper.

She shot him a toothy grin, now darkened by a slash of melted black crumbs. "Kit cat?"

Along with a handkerchief to wipe up the worst of the chocolate, he took a comb from his pocket to do something with her tufts of curls. "Yep, Gnat Nat, you're going to see the kitty. Let's hope we don't get our eyes scratched out."

Greezy. Damn. He'd forgotten his allergy medication. "That'll work to our benefit. I am worth my salt, you know."

Kent collected the diaper bag. He got Natalie into her stroller, then hefted a sack of groceries and made for the duplex. Whatever it took, he'd turn showtime into success city.

This was not going well.

Seeing Natalie again was just as bad as Caroline Grant had imagined it. No. Worse. This time she knew about the tyke's affliction, and each time she toppled, or got excited, Caroline figured this was it. The child's heart would play out.

Kent, poor man, couldn't stop sneezing. Greezy wouldn't vacate the kitchen, and attempts to lock her in the bedroom only resulted in feline caterwauling that neither Kent nor Caroline could take.

And, to top it off, he'd lied—at home in front of a range, he wasn't.

Kent scorched macaroni and cheese. He singed the fried shrimp. English peas turned mushy from too much boiling in too much water and a stick of butter, the real kind. That meal had enough cholesterol to send a heart patient to the emergency room.

To Caroline's relief, he'd brought a couple of jars of baby food. This afternoon, when the visiting nurse saw to her patient's comfort, she asked the no-nonsense brunette about heart conditions in babies. The child needed to be under a doctor's care, not dragged all over Texas, looking for shelter.

While Kent set the table, Caroline decided to make a concession. "You must take that baby back to Dallas right away. Settle her in somewhere. Do exactly as the doctor orders. I—I'll make certain I'm there for the surgery. Somehow."

His brow lowering, he arranged silverware just so. "Uh, about that—"

"Kent, you're a sweetheart," she interrupted. "But what must be done, must be done."

"I— You—" A sneeze clamped his remark. Afterward, he didn't look at her as he asked, "What if she didn't need surgery? What if she just needs a sister?"

"I'll be there for the surgery. That's all."

"I suppose I ought to be thankful for small favors."

As Caroline looked at it, he expected the world where Natalie was concerned. But seeing him with the child gave the impression Baby meant a lot to him.

How refreshing, being with a man who liked children.

After the last of the baby food had been consumed and the adults had picked at their less-than-delicious meal, Greezy chose to roost on his lap.

Eyes watery and swollen, Kent announced, "Need something for my allergies. Gotta go—ahh-choo!—to the drugstore."

"There's one not more than a block from your hotel. I'm sure it's still open.'' Better he and the frail baby should leave and allow Caroline to get accustomed to her promise.

Another attack of sneezes into a tissue. ''I can't drive with her, not like this. I'll have to leave her here.''

Caroline fixed eyes on the girl who'd climbed to the sofa and was half-asleep. Sheer terror jabbed. ''I—I don't know the first thing about babies. I don't even like kids!''

''Not true,'' he came back, sniffling.

''Okay, I do like kids. But I don't want dependents.''

Blinking several times, he asked, ''Is that why you and Frank didn't have kids?''

''A good lawyer never asks a question without knowing the answer. You talked to Ruth. She talked to Frank. So answer your own question.''

''I didn't ask as an attorney. I don't know the answer.''

Unwilling to acknowledge her own heart, she replied, ''Children aren't part of my plan.''

''You don't want your, your—ahhchoo!''

''Greezy, get out of the man's face.''

She didn't, of course. Kent craned his neck around a flat, mottled head to say, ''I need drugs. Now.''

''You can't leave Natalie here. Anything could happen. She might have a heart attack!''

''Ahh-choo!'' Kent snapped up another tissue and shoved Greezy off his lap. ''What if I have a wreck?''

''You'd better not crash your car. If you do, I'm calling Child Protective Services. First thing.''

Oh, no. She'd agreed to baby-sit!

Kent, without another word, slipped out the front door, then locked it with a borrowed key.

Things went well for the next thirty minutes. Natalie fell asleep amid a nest of couch pillows and snoozed peacefully, and Caroline studied the tyke.

What a pretty child. The au pair had dressed her in a darling romper, although it had chocolate stains on the front. Were babies supposed to eat chocolate?

Baby also had a double row of dark lashes that swept down on pudgy cheeks, and a mouth like the angels depicted in the stained glass of the church George Danson had taken his daughter to.

Maternal instincts surfaced, her fingers itching to brush the hair that grew too long on a tiny forehead. Natalie needed either a barrette or bangs.

Some of Caroline's most cherished memories had been French-braiding her stepdaughter's hair. They had both enjoyed those times. Quality time. What sort of quality time, if any, had Natalie known?

How had Ruth treated this baby?

One thing was obvious. Ruth hadn't thought enough to stay in the same country with the child she'd gone to such lengths to bring into the world. Earlier, Kent had said the Perrys were in deepest Africa, on a photographic odyssey to Timbuktu, when they had contracted a killer disease.

Ruth hadn't changed.

"I bet she never once worried about Baby's condition."

Caroline's strident tone startled Natalie. She flinched as if struck, eyes popping open to widen with disorientation and dismay. The cat flew from the sofa when the baby screamed.

"Don't you dare have a heart attack," Caroline barked.

Natalie screamed louder, fists flailing. She coughed.

"No, Baby. No. It's going to be okay." That was all Caroline could think to do, plead for sanity. What did one do for a pint-size invalid? "Shh. Kent's coming back. He'll be back in a minute. Everything's going to be all right."

"No, no, no, no." Natalie jerked upward, twisted her body. Pillows flew. She fell to the floor with a heart-stopping thud, before Caroline could reach her.

She tried hard to reach her. The cast got in the way. Natalie continued to scream at the top of her lungs, losing her breath. At last Caroline gripped little arms. Clumsy, she was. Somehow she situated Natalie on her lap. But the girl sought to twist away.

"I won't drop you," Caroline crooned, trying to convince herself as well as her charge. "Shh."

She didn't know what else to do but sing. Daddy had sung to her, what seemed like ninety years ago. She couldn't remember any tunes but those made popular by a group of head-bangers, one of her stepdaughter's favorites.

A singer, Caroline was not.

Greezy darted from behind the TV, raised her hackles and hissed. Young eyes went wide again. This time with disbelief. That was when Natalie gagged. Gagged, then vomited.

Caroline let loose with a swear word that she hoped Baby would never, ever repeat, provided she lived. What to do now? Call 911. The phone? Out of reach. Nothing close by for clean-up. Where was that long-handled picker thing the nurse had delivered? In the bedroom. Naturally.

Plaintive baby sobs tearing at her, Caroline tried to wheel toward the telephone. Impossible. She couldn't hold this dying child and wheel, too. But she must do *something*.

"Hush, Natalie Perry. Hush. Don't you dare die. You've got to help me think this thing through. Let me hold you close."

She lifted Natalie against a shoulder.

Thankfully, the baby hiccuped, then eased down. She didn't quit crying, but arms folded around Caroline's neck; the elder of Ruth's girls, meanwhile, got hold of a crutch. Still, the phone eluded her. It took maneuvering, but she inched the tissue box to the wheel of her chair. After two tries, she had it.

Caroline dragged in a breath. "Let's get you sopped up, okay? That's a good girl. That's a real good girl. I've gotta wipe your nose—it's running. There. That's better. Why am I worried about a runny nose?" She wadded up the tissues. "Now, hang on tight, Angel Baby. We've got to get this doggone wheelchair over to the phone."

Natalie nestled. Scaling Mount Everest had to be easier than crossing this room, but Caroline made it. At last she had a means of rescue in hand. Before she could punch the first digit of the emergency number, Baby grabbed the phone.

"F-fon. Fon." The receiver upside down to her mouth, she smiled and showed six teeth. A squeal of delight filled the air. "Kenn…Kenn."

"You're not dying." Caroline sighed in relief, looping her arms around Angel Baby and giving a series of kisses to her forehead. "Everything is going to be just fine."

* * *

This was what Kent Mackay had hoped for, an aspect of family unity. He grinned. Big. Then pulled the front door gently closed. There they were, Caroline's back to him, holding her sister.

Natalie was gazing rapturously into her sister's eyes.

His chest puffed. His orphan-charge was on her way to a home. And he'd be back in Dallas in no time, mission accomplished.

Meanwhile, he'd correct her sister's overblown ideas about the medical condition. *Hold on, Mackay. You don't know Gnat Nat will be all right.*

He stepped toward the twosome, halting next to the TV that blared cartoons. "Sorry it took so long. A wreck had McCullough Avenue closed, and I got lost taking a detour."

"You." Caroline snapped a glower at him. "You!" Her hand grabbed a crutch. She hoisted it. It went flying.

At Kent. He ducked.

The crutch tip conked Greezy. "Eeoww!" She flew from atop the TV and lunged for Kent, claws digging his shoulder.

"Get off!"

He yelled those words as he picked at feline legs attached to material and his flesh. Claws dug deeper. Hair standing on its end, Greezy bit him. A comical woodpecker in the cartoon gave a series of gleeful, staccato cackles, as if taking personal delight in the attack that didn't cease.

Yelping again, Kent at last shook off his attacker, who beat for the bedroom.

And Caroline and Natalie were laughing.

He sneezed, the antihistamines obviously not having had time to work.

This was *not* what he'd hoped for.

"What was the meaning of that?" His question, asked into a tissue, had a stiff edge to it.

"It's for dumping a dying child on me."

He studied Natalie. "She looks fine. Except for— What's on her clothes? And yours?"

"Her dinner." Caroline slid fingers beneath Natalie's armpits and boosted her in Kent's direction. "Take her."

He did as ordered. Natalie tugged on his scratched shoulder and giggled. Whatever had happened, she seemed okay. He took it upon himself to go to the bedroom, to scowl at the cat perched on a far windowsill, then to snatch a blanket. Thereafter, he returned to make a pallet and settle Natalie on it. But not before he tuned out the mocking woodpecker.

A music channel, the soft one, gave forth romantic tunes.

Supplies snagged from the diaper bag, Kent set about righting Baby. Off with soiled clothes and soggy diaper. Some well-placed swipes with a wet wipe. Baby powder. Diaper on. Gown slipped over her head. He loved taking care of Natalie.

"What, no bottle?" Caroline asked as he sat Indian-style on the floor to cradle and rock her sister.

"No bottle. It might upset her tummy."

"You know a great deal about kids."

"I'm winging it."

By now Natalie was sleeping again. Content. As if nothing had happened earlier. He eased her to the makeshift bed and tucked a blanket under her chin.

A song about loving lies wafted around them as

Caroline spoke. "You're wonderful with her. Except for what you'd have fed her at suppertime. Cholesterol is bad for her heart condition."

That. Damn. If there ever were a time to equivocate, it was now. "There weren't any chapters in the book, dealing with sickly babies. But I don't doubt you're right."

Silence drifted down, filtering into a provocative tune from the TV, the perfect kind for dirty dancing. He sensed Caroline's eyes on him. What was she thinking?

"Some lucky woman will count her stars, having you to father her children."

Her words landed with the force of a meteor, crushing and burning his insides. There would be no children for Kent Mackay. He would never have kids of his own.

He snapped off the TV.

The room's light faded without warning. Caroline had switched the lamp to dim, and he was damned glad for that, since he didn't wish to show his expression.

Her voice floated like morning mist. "I've been saving a bottle of white Zinfandel for emergencies. If you're interested, it's in the fridge."

He got the wine.

Neither spoke until half the contents were down weary throats. Caroline broke the silence. Rubbing the wineglass's lip, she said, "I'm sorry about the crutch. My temper got away from me. You have to understand, I thought Natalie was dying. She woke up terrified, started screaming, turned blue."

She'd done that, more than once, since he'd taken

custody, although the au pair had chalked it up to temper tantrums. "She, uh, misses her mother."

"How can that be? I don't know much about babies, but I think I know the problem. She never knows what to expect. There's no permanency in her life. No continuity."

"That's what I've been trying to tell you."

"I won't lie to you," Caroline whispered. "I feel terrible for her. Alone in the world, no one to love her."

Two peas in a pod, Ruth's daughters. He decided against voicing that remark.

"No one to love her, Kent. No one but you."

A string pulled in his heart. "I hope that'll change."

"I know you do, I know you do."

He ventured a glance at Caroline. Her poignant mien pulled another of his heart strings. Hers was a lovely face.

"What's the chance we can work something out?" he asked.

"I'm not fit to raise her. That little thing needs more than I can give. More than you can give, too. Baby needs a steadying influence. Or she'll carry no telling what kind of emotional scars into adulthood. She needs more than a sister. She needs a mother."

It was his turn for sarcasm. "Got any idea where I can search? I'm not familiar with the San Antonio classifieds."

Caroline lessened the space between them. "I'll bet anything you could break Don's will, where she can be adopted. I also think you exaggerated, saying no one would want her. Many couples would do anything to adopt such a beautiful child. Her bad heart won't hold them back."

Wiping a hand down his mustache, he said, "Natalie does have a lot going in the cute department."

"Why did you exaggerate? For my benefit? Or for some other reason?" Wisdom in her expression, she said, "I'd bank on the latter. There's something about you, something that hurts you deeply."

Awed by her perception, he answered slowly, "Could be."

"What is it? Not being reared by your parents?"

He never talked about his younger years. Settling back against the sofa, he considered sidestepping her question, yet for some strange reason, he felt compelled to honesty. "My mother skipped out of the hospital, once she got a look at me. My father never bothered to take a look. No one wanted a boy with a..." *A disfigured boy.* "I wasn't appealing."

He'd remained unappealing, even after corrective surgery that should have been done in his infancy. He'd been in school before the State approved payment for the procedure. Six years old and scarred for life, inside and out.

"I never fit in." He'd known a succession of institutions and foster homes; a speech impediment that took years to overcome had furthered his bitterness, had secured his place in the caste of untouchables. "It was a truant officer who opened the world for me, by sticking my nose in books."

Caroline studied him for what seemed like hours, but must have been limited to moments. "You're handsome. You must have been a darling boy. Why wouldn't someone want you as their son?"

He jackknifed to stand. Pacing the floor and steering past the cast, he frowned. Why had he opened his mouth? Furthermore, he didn't like being exposed like this, bloodied on the rocks of memories.

"It's past nine," he muttered. "Time to get Natalie back to the hotel."

"Not yet. I need you. I need you to talk to me."

That she could admit need chipped at the invisible wall that he'd built around himself. He halted in front of her wheelchair to peer down into compassionate eyes. Oddly, it was easier to speak than he'd imagined. "It took surgery to correct my problem. A mustache to hide the scar."

Caroline lifted upturned hands to him. Her tawny face budded into a smile of understanding. "Come here."

"No."

"Sit down, right here in front of me. Humor me."

Her voice, so mellow yet insistent, drew him. He hunkered down, his gaze arrowing to her face. The light from the kitchen made a corona around the long gold hair that hid her shoulders.

"Come closer, Kent."

He braced his hands beside her hips, and she took his jaws between her palms to draw him nearer. His heart gave an extra beat, when her thumb trailed to his mustache, and began to lift it. He jerked away, prisoner to yesteryears. She wouldn't let go. Tenderness in her eyes, she ran that thumb along the white line left by the surgery to correct his cleft palate.

And then she raised her lips to the whiskers hiding the scar. A shudder went through him as she gentled a kiss to the place that sent his parents scurrying from the hospital.

When Caroline straightened, she spoke softly,

sweetly. "I think you're wonderful, Kent Mackay. You ought to, too."

This was the first time in his life that he, a magna cum laude graduate of law school and litigation master at the Hardwicke Law Firm, had ever felt total acceptance.

He cupped Caroline's face between his hands, the fine strands of the hair at her temples tickling his fingertips. Warmth swirled and built to a yearning in his groin. His lips pressed hers, taking more than he should. Her arms slipped up his back. She tasted of wine, tenderness and promise as she gave herself to their kiss. Caroline was a balm to the soul, one he'd spent thirty years looking for.

It was then that Ruth's baby let out a piercing cry, yanking Kent back to reality.

What was he going to do about Natalie?

For the little girl, and for himself, he intended to stick around and explore the possibilities with Caroline.

Chapter Four

"I've done it now, Greezy."

The tortoiseshell, perched on the kitchen windowsill stopped eyeing a cardinal outside, and swiveled to give Caroline a crossed-eyed, insolent glare.

"I've said that at least twice today, ever since Kent and Natalie accepted my invitation." Caroline Grant, ignoring her leg injury, wheeled closer. "If you had brains beyond oral gratification, you'd know I said the same thing last night."

Presently, Kent and Natalie were in the bedroom, where he endeavored to get the baby down for an afternoon nap.

"Oh, Greezy, what am I going to do?"

The tortie licked a paw, then groomed an ear.

Actually, Caroline didn't regret having given comfort to Kent. She knew what it was like, having no support system. She'd never had one herself, yet she often gave tender mercies such as she'd been denied. Usually her weakness was used against her.

"I wonder how many hearts Kent's broken with his story of being rejected?"

Recalling a comment he'd made on judging his deeds, Caroline knew it wasn't fair to assume anything about his love life. After all, he had claimed to be too busy for one. "Anyhow, I like that man. He seems honest, trustworthy. Sensitive to the needs of others. And he's been hurt, just as I have. Like Natalie has."

Impervious to the suffering of humans, the haughty cat left her roost no doubt to inspect, and pilfer from, the cardboard box that Caroline opened.

"Oh, no, you don't. Don't you dare jump on the table."

Lifting pastries from the box—a hostess gift, Kent had called these fruit tarts—Caroline arranged them on one of the stiff disposable plates he'd also provided. The adults intended to laze over dessert, once Natalie got to sleep.

"Here I am, sweet on a guy as well as Ruth's baby." Would she ever forget the feel of his mink-soft mustache, his fine lips or the sensations that frenzied from the touch of his hands? "It got wild last night."

Greezy's "murr-ow" didn't sound a bit like "You should be careful," but those were the words that went through Caroline's head.

Centering the filled plate on the bean-bag-bottomed lap tray that had been yet another part of the never-ending Mackay bounty that included electronic air cleaners for each room of the duplex, Caroline wheeled from the kitchen. Just days ago, she'd never accepted anyone's help, yet her humble home brimmed with helpful things. Including a fine man who touched her soft center.

It was enough to make her forget an itching, aching leg.

How much she would give to Natalie remained to be seen, but accepting a plethora of goods was a trade-off. Goods for services.

For the next few days she and Kent would accord Natalie a semblance of security. Doing so, they would decide the course of the child's future. No mean feat.

Caroline had no idea how to tap-dance, when she couldn't even stand. How could she waltz past her attraction to Kent, provide for a sister and do her job at the same time? Fill-Er-Fast had to be top priority. Her analyses had to be compiled, cast or no cast.

Oh, for a decent computer. Data delivered by snail mail, or downloaded to the information back road of Mr. Ugly, made it difficult, turning that data into clear-cut reports.

Kent, on the other hand, had made the transition with ease. Last night, after leaving here, he took Natalie to an emergency clinic; she hadn't suffered a heart seizure.

Today he'd cleared his calendar. Already he'd sent the au pair to London. Already he'd checked out of the hotel. Already his suitcase and Angel Baby's assorted gear were settled in the duplex, an agreement between him and the hostess that he'd sleep on the sofa.

On the sofa, not far from Caroline's bed.

She'd really done it now.

The pastry plate left behind, Caroline wheeled past air cleaners and toward her bedroom, halting short of the doorway. Like the wheels that had taken her across these hardwood floors but were now locked, her breath stopped. Kent didn't have Natalie in the crib. Eyes closed, Greezy a ball at his feet, he rested in the middle of George Danson's old iron-frame bed—Caroline's bed—Baby cuddled to his side.

Something vital went through Caroline, something that caressed her with a thrill as she gazed at him, a shiver that allowed flat-out pleasure.

He inhabited satin sheets and comforter, her one extravagance. His left arm held the little girl who had newly cut bangs. And his arm was bare...like his bronzed chest. He had an interesting pattern to the fine, black hairs that swirled on a first-class set of pectorals, that pelt meandering below the top snap of his jeans. How could anyone think him less than male perfection?

Yet cat scratches marred his shoulder. He'd taken that attack well, all things considered. He had a great attitude. And he was fantastic with kisses.

Good-looking, easy-charm Kent was a pro at kissing. He hadn't gotten that from kissing a pig. He'd been practicing on women. And if he wasn't to be believed about how busy work kept him, there might be a trail of broken hearts in his wake.

A chilling thought.

He began to stir, his head moving to the side, his lips opening to swallow. Without conscious thought, he resettled the slumbering babe to the crook of that hairy arm.

Man and child.

Right there amid Caroline's satin sheets.

She knew what a man's scent did to a bed. Tonight, when she went there, the door closed between her and temptation, she would smell sandalwood and man. How would she handle it?

Back-wheeling and turning the chair away from the doorway, she was nonetheless alerted to the possibility that he hadn't been sleeping when she'd gawked. The springs squeaked.

"I used your bed for a couple of winks," he said from behind her in a low, smooth voice. "I figured to get Gnat Nat sleepy-eyed by holding her. Worked for me, too."

Caroline glanced backward. He stood just inside the living room, giving her an eyeful of a first-class breadth of chest.

"Baby might smother in all that chest hair of yours," she accused.

"Like it?"

Why wouldn't he be confident of his appeal? Last night she'd made it known. The wounded child in his spirit needed bolstering, and it still did.

As for herself, honesty was important to Caroline. If he didn't ascribe to it she could career herself down the garden path. A succession of women may have been meant to mend the broken child while having their hearts stolen by the handsome man.

"I should imagine Natalie likes your furry pillow enough for both of us," she answered. "Where is she?"

"Sleeping in her crib."

Over and above Caroline's collective doubts, she added another and expressed it. "How is it that you can just hang around here? Don't you have work to do, or something?"

"I have a heavy caseload. But I have a junior attorney, and law clerks, to help out. Natalie Perry is my most important client at the moment. It's my duty to see to her comforts and needs, since she can't look out for herself. I wouldn't be much of a lawyer if I washed my hands of her. And I'd be betraying a trust to her late father. I promised Don I'd give the trusteeship my best, till she's an adult.''

That sounded reasonable to Caroline.

A grin tilted the edges of Kent's mustache. ''Besides, I'm long overdue for a break from the office. You're a great break, Caro.''

Just don't break my heart.

He scooted around her chair. ''Ah, I see you got our dessert. Is the coffee brewed?'' Apparently the latter needed no answer, since he headed into the kitchen and returned with saucers balanced in each sizable palm.

''Ready for a treat?'' He bent to place one coffee on the low table, giving Caroline a whiff of sandalwood-scented man, reminding her of those sheets in the bedroom.

Kent handed her the other saucer and cup, his fingers whisking against the heel of her palm, as if he didn't know what his touch did to her. Maybe he did. Of course he did.

''What are you thinking?'' He eased onto the sofa to kick bare heels up on a hassock. Those were long feet.

She couldn't mention that she was trying to analyze his shoe size.

However, she could say honestly, ''I'll be blunt with you, Kent Mackay. I'm thinking I'm in a fine mess. I could get attached to that baby, but I know you're banking on that.'' *I could get attached to you, too.*

His eyes sparkled with unrepentant blue glee. "What's wrong with that?"

"I could end up...I might end up..."

"End up feeling empty, played out? Lonesome and alone?"

"Wait just a minute, Mackay. Just because I'm crippled until mid-August doesn't mean I don't have a life."

He bit into a fruit tart, chewing slowly, obviously pondering her words. After swallowing a sip of coffee, he said, "So, working nine to five is enough for you?"

How could she know? She hadn't been with Fill-Er-Fast long enough to know how it would go. But it had better go like gasoline during the summer season, or else the flare of her career might flicker. That was too scary to contemplate.

"Isn't your legal practice enough for you?" she challenged.

"Lawyers don't make it big by twiddling their thumbs."

She studied those thumbs. They were well kept and lacked the calluses formed by gripping monkey wrenches. These hands were every bit as broad as Frank's. These fingers were longer, were studded with wisps of crisp black hairs. These hands belonged to a man who'd struggled out of the mire of a bad childhood, had held books to educate their owner. They had...well, no telling where those hands had been over the years.

How educated were they in the craft of making love?

You are a sex-starved piece of work, she admonished herself. This attraction needed to stop. It wasn't his nebulous love life that worried her as much as the obvious: they were no match. Her life was here, his in Dallas.

But could impulses be trained?

Taking a swallow of coffee, she forced a question about his occupation. "Just how big are you?"

Too bad her gaze was trained somewhat south of his face, since he chuckled and answered in a timbre that didn't mistake his meaning. "I size up."

"Braggart," she accused, before steering him to her designed course. "How much money do you make off Baby?"

"Four hundred an hour."

"Four hundred, times all these hours in San Antonio!"

"Don't forget travel time. Or office hours. By the way, I got a third of Don's settlement. That's standard."

Irked, she wouldn't ask how much money Natalie had. It was beneath her. "What about overtime?"

"Hourly workers make overtime, not lawyers."

"Cold comfort. No wonder you expect me to mooch off my sister."

"Don't look at me like that. She'll never miss the money." He stretched, showing off his attributes.

They didn't look quite so good now. Caroline got an icky feeling. She remembered what it was like, having someone siphon off money, like Ruth had with Daddy's insurance money. Someone needed to protect Natalie from siphon hoses.

"Discounting thirds," Caroline enumerated, "let's say you work a normal year. You could bill eight-hundred, thirty-two thousand *a year* to Baby."

"That's hypothetical. I'm not making a career off Natalie Perry, nor do I toil every hour. Besides, her investments bring in more than enough to cover my charges.''

"What a guy."

"I'll waive my fees, if you take her permanently."

"I could stomp your toes."

"You can't," he pointed out. "You're crippled."

"That is especially insensitive, coming from you."

A grin as wide as the state of Texas spread across his mustached face. "Get rid of the cast, and I'll take you on."

"What's the use of arguing with a professional debater?"

"Let's put the professional aside...."

How could she? He'd made a success of himself, had done it without too much effort, it seemed. Here he was, younger than Caroline, yet he had long ago shaken off poverty and its appurtenances. And here she was, a woman from the wrong side of Pasadena, still cloaked in it.

Well, he hadn't spent years shelling peas, washing socks and yanking valves in a refinery. Anyone could make it big, provided he had drive, opportunity and a helpless little girl to fatten his bank account.

Rather than stew over those, Caroline recalled their discussion, before it had taken this shift. "I'll grant you're a busy, successful lawyer. I'll be busy, too, once I return to Fill-Er-Fast."

"Get serious. You won't burn the midnight oil, finding ways to keep the price of gasoline out the ceiling. You're not so busy that you can't make room for...other things."

His remark wormed up her spine. While the gist was different, Kent's was the sort of remark that Frank would have made. Any and everything was more important than her career. A woman's place was to shell peas, go to a menial job; and when the refinery shift was over, make everything comfortable for someone else. In Frank's case, that meant Frank.

This kind of scorning, mercenary sex appeal, to Caroline's ears, reminded her of the dweeb she'd finally gotten enough of.

"You're angry," Kent assessed aloud.

"Why don't you just eat that fruit tart, and hush up?"

He had the audacity to laugh.

Somewhere Kent had made a wrong move, and it had something to do with Caroline's job or his fees. Or both. Her frosty gaze, when she wasn't ignoring him, stated no interest in discussing the subject. Mixed signals, that was what he got from Caroline. Strange, how she could reach out with her heart one minute, then retreat the next.

The rest of that afternoon she eyeballed Mr. Ugly's screen. Kent and Natalie might not have been in the room, for all the attention she gave them, even when their game of hide-and-seek got out of hand. The baby grabbed a handful of reports; they went flying.

"Ignore me, if you please, Caro. But Gnat Nat needs your attention."

"Gotta work," she mumbled and tapped a key that started her dot-matrix printer.

He waited a few minutes, then stacked the fallen reports by Mr. Ugly. This was the first time in three hours Kent had gotten a whiff of Caroline's perfume that would tempt a monk.

No, it wasn't the perfume. It's what Caroline did for it. He'd smelled that fragrance before. The senior partner at the firm wore it, but Lorraine Hardwicke never smelled this good.

With Natalie tugging on his jeans leg, he said to her sister, "Any chance we can call a truce?"

Caroline punched a series of keys, the screen becoming a black sea of fish rather than columns of figures. "I'm too disgusted with you for a truce."

She'd be even more disgusted if she knew... When he took Natalie to the emergency clinic, the doctor had checked her ticker. Nothing wrong with Baby's heart. He hadn't sent Natalie to a hospital or ordered medication, which went along with Dr. McBride's earlier report. Apparently Natalie had outgrown her problem.

Nevertheless, Kent had paid the bill and asked the receptionist to send a copy of the report to the Dallas pediatrician.

While his continued ruse shamed Kent, he wouldn't cut it short, not with things as they were. But he wasn't lying when he said, "It's not good for Gnat Nat, having tension between us."

"Natalie isn't the only person involved here. And this person doesn't appreciate your dissing her career."

So that was it, the job angle. "Will you accept my apologies? I honestly didn't mean to offend you."

She allowed Natalie to crawl on her lap. Her arms going around the toddler, she said, "What did you mean?"

"I was trying to point out—aw, hell, Caroline, I want you to have time for me and Gnat Nat. That's what I meant."

"Don't curse around this baby." Her hands cupped Natalie's young ears.

Kent smothered a grin. Having Caroline again show

interest was just the ticket. Now all he needed to do
was recapture her attention in a certain Dallas lawyer.

No, that was not all Kent needed to do. At seven
that evening, right after he'd bathed Natalie, Caroline
had a visitor. Filmore Wanek, Operations Director for
Fill-Er-Fast, dropped in. Kent had long known the gas-
oline-retailer chain had a lousy reputation, but he
naively expected more out of its executives.

Filmore Wanek barged in to traverse the living
room, his patent-leather-shod feet echoing on the hardwood floor. Those were almost dainty feet. They
didn't match Wanek's florid face, his elevated height
nor his sizable middle.

Frankly, Kent had never seen a man, not even a bail
bondsman, in such a combination of plaids, none of
which matched. The cheap trousers and sports coat did
go right along with Wanek's ambience, though.

While Kent, in a chair beside the sofa, continued to
size up Caroline's "superior" and shoved Natalie's
arms into her sleeper, Wanek ranted and raved about
Fill-Er-Fast being undercut in the San Antonio market
by the reputable Emerald Clover chain. He segued to,
"When you gonna be outta that chair, gal?"

Kent took note of her expression. She might not
have a problem with labels like "gal," but she clearly
didn't appreciate the tone behind Wanek's "gal."
Kent didn't like it, either.

He nestled Natalie against his chest, wishing he
could do the same for Caroline, while Wanek went on.
"Get on crutches or something. We need you at the
office."

"I'm not good with crutches. And my doctor says
I must rest with my leg elevated. There's no couch in

the ladies' room at work. There's nowhere to prop my cast. And I'm working here. If I need to do more, I will."

"I like to see the whites of my crew's eyes when they're working." Wanek slashed the heel of his hand through the air. "Hike that leg up on your desk, gal. That's what you can do."

That was when Kent spoke. "Hold up, partner. Ms. Grant won't be hiking her leg on any desk. And, furthermore, what's this about no place for the ladies to rest in your offices? I thought a couch was standard practice for companies, nowadays."

Wanek turned beady little eyes on him. "Who're you?"

"Like Ms. Grant told you, had you been listening," Kent reintroduced himself. "I'm a houseguest."

Wanek plucked a cigar from the inside of his gaudy sports coat, but had the grace—or was it for the lack of a match?—not to light up. He rolled the stogie from one side of his thick lips to the other. "Who's the kid?"

"She's my sister." Caroline palmed her ponytail. "She's visiting for a few days."

"Sister?" Wanek took a gander at the child who listened from the cradle of Kent's arms. "Well, if that don't beat all. Kinda looks like you, she does." He actually smiled, but the moment was broken by his modifier. "Kinda fat."

The cool attorney within Kent transposed to a beast, and he had the overwhelming urge to give Wanek a taste of his fist. He even reared up a few inches. No one was going to disparage his women. But one look from Caroline curbed his instincts. She had a don't-you-dare look in her eyes.

"'Course, I always liked corn-fed heifers." Wanek plopped down on the sofa. "Just more of 'em to love."

"Say one more word, partner, and I'll advise Ms. Grant to file a sexual-harassment charge against you."

"Oh, Kent, no! Just hush. Please."

At Caroline's elevated voice, Natalie sat up.

"If this don't beat all. I come here to tell you something good, gal, and what do I get?" Wanek thumped his chest with the tip of a forefinger, the unlit cigar dancing between that finger and the third one. "Threatened."

"I said nothing of the kind, Filmore. And I speak for myself. Don't listen to Mr. Mackay."

That in itself got under Kent's skin, but he approached her remark as an attorney. Blandly. Besides, reason told him Caroline was scared of losing her job. What would it take to convince her into another one?

Filmore Wanek settled down to say, "One of the boys may be out the door. I might move you into his slot. 'Course, it'll mean traveling. And a heap more work to take care of. But it's got a raise attached. Why, it's an out-and-out promotion."

Her face brightened with excitement.

Kent scowled.

It gnawed at him, the future. Caroline, putting up with Filmore Wanek. Caroline, moving ahead in a company that had elevated Filmore Wanek to the executive-washroom level. Caroline Grant was too good for him.

But she would stay with the company; Kent knew it, now that a carrot had been dangled in front of her nose.

There would be no time for Natalie, or for a lonely

Dallas attorney. Unless Kent could convince her of a few facts. Like, how her career had done little in her time of need, after the accident. Fill-Er-Fast paid the bills, yes—no small thing—but who'd saved her from Dominick's All The Way?

Tonight was certainly not the night for convincing, not with Caroline eyeing that carrot like a hungry mare.

Kent rose from the chair, picked Natalie up and headed for the bedroom, closing the door behind them. He settled the cherub in bed, but she would have none of that.

She stood, extending her arms. "'Tory."

"Right. Bedtime story."

He found a book about a spotted dog who always returned to the sheltering paws of his mommy. But he closed the book way before Mommy corralled Spotty. Kent brushed fingertips along Natalie's fine hair. "I've got it bad for your sister."

Natalie gnawed on the baby-bed rail.

"What I need is a woman who'll understand me. Your sister could be the one. She accepts me, flaws and all." Kissing his upper lip had unmasked the real Caroline, the tender woman beneath her sharp camouflage. Kent could read juries. Judges. Defendants and plaintiffs. He trusted his instincts.

But what if she knew the whole story? The entire nasty story of Kent Mackay? Phooey. The issue would never come up.

"I may have fallen a little bit in love with her last night," he said to Natalie. "Not that I know what love is."

His experiences had followed the stages of his life. A youth's experiments. A young man's fantasies turned to reality. Then the urge to settle down. That third stage—forget it. His fourth stage, rife with fantasy and feeling, might be the sort to hang on to.

"We're kindred spirits, the three of us. Yes, three. We need each other. Best of all, she's made it clear— becoming a mother isn't important to her. That fits my plans. No kids."

On that he was adamant.

Okay, Gerrie Gale, Natalie's former au pair, claimed he was a "born father," but that was beside the point.

"Let's not give up on your sister just yet." And he was moving too fast. "We did get this invitation, you know." He patted Natalie's arm. "I intend to utilize these days. For you, for me. And for your sister."

Thank heavens, Caroline was finally alone. Once Filmore Wanek left, she'd counted the minutes until bedtime, and had praised her lucky stars when Kent suggested moving the portable crib into the living room, closer to him.

Alone, she struggled into nightclothes, then wheeled over to gaze at the moon from her bedroom window. She ought not to rhapsodize over her prospects at Fill-Er-Fast. But she did. Filmore Wanek was a boor, a bore and hostile, but she'd known worse at the refinery. She would rise above Wanek. Maybe even take *his* job someday.

A grin poked at her face, as she recalled Kent's reaction to her boss's outdated ways. It was new to her, having someone to champion her. New and not altogether loathsome. Yet she would make a name for herself without anyone's help.

"I can't have Kent interfering with my job," she

whispered. "Fill-Er-Fast gave me a chance, and I won't let Filmore Wanek down."

Her eyes on the clotted clouds that moved over the moon, she dreamed of the future. At last, after thirty-one years, she was going somewhere. A promotion! It could happen.

"Someday I'll be bragging on my accomplishments."

Greezy chose to vault into her lap.

Caroline glanced down and saw an unhappy mug. "You don't like being shut away from that baby, do you?"

The tortie hopped down and sashayed to the doorway. Butt hiked up, tail even higher, she pushed her nose beneath the door.

"Greezy Althea Victoria Regina, get over here," Caroline muttered below the air cleaner's whir. A loud coo might work. "Come to Momma, sweetie."

A voice, male as all get out, filtered from the closed portal between here and the living room cum guest quarters. "Caro honey, did you call me?"

Caro honey?

"No, Kent. I didn't. Greezy wants Baby. That's all."

"I don't think Gnat Nat would mind...."

"She's my cat."

"Natalie is your sister."

Caroline grabbed the bamboo back scratcher that had Korea '52 burned into its handle, and tossed it toward the door. It pinged impotently against wood. "Go away, Mackay."

"Ineffectual means bring ineffectual results." He thumped the door once. "Want a knife to throw at me?"

"Yes!"

In that easy style of his, he simply laughed. Laughed in a winsome way Filmore Wanek aspired to but couldn't get right, even if he lived to be a hundred. There were men, and there were men. Wanek and Mackay would never be confused.

Strange...

Oh, yes, it was strange, the butter that melted through Caroline. She wanted that infuriating man. Wanted Kent badly. Or dearly. Or heartily. Or whatever. She also wanted to go places with Fill-Er-Fast, but that was beside the point. Being cloaked in hairy arms, having a decent man fly to her defense, held more appeal than a woman ought to allow.

Are you nuts? He's a control freak. He could be a regression to less enlightened times, even more so than her boss. And she couldn't forget that Kent lived off Baby, at least part-time, and his experience with kisses hadn't come from swine.

Then she approached the iron bed, where Kent had rested his head this afternoon, where his scent lingered. There was nothing to do but struggle between those sheets. And when she did, the faint scent of him got to her.

"Oh, man, I am in trouble," Caroline whispered, realizing impulses could *never* be trained.

"Kent, help me!"

He charged into Caroline's bedroom with the speed of EMS, and switched on the light. "What's wrong?"

"My leg. It itches."

A mass of misery, she reclined in that big old bed. A beautiful mass of misery, she was, her hair a cloud around her shoulders, her thin nightgown clinging to lush curves. Her eyes had the look of a little girl who had tried and failed.

"I can't reach my back scratcher," she said. "Would you mind handing it here? It's on the floor, somewhere."

Already he'd crunched the thing under his big foot. One hand grabbed the broken tool. "I, uh, no problem." He advanced. "I'd like to scratch your itch."

"I don't mean *that*."

He hadn't necessarily meant a double entendre, but what the hell? "Don't ever downplay your itches, Caro. Not when you have someone to scratch them. Let me."

"If this was another day and time, I'd call you a rogue."

"I'm not bothered by labels," he responded, throwing her own phraseology back at her.

He reached the bed, the springs protesting as he sat on the edge. Springs? He could imagine them singing. Caroline was nowhere near the singing stage. "How can I be of service?"

"My ankle. My knee. Oh, hell, Kent, all of it! I just want to scratch and scratch. I don't know what to do. Help me!"

He glanced at the broken bamboo device. "I'll get a coat hanger. Please tell me you have wire ones."

"I have wire coat hangers."

"Not to beat me with, I trust," he teased.

"You must've watched that Joan Crawford movie."

"At midnight one night."

Silence, followed by Caroline's, "Do you watch many movies with chicks?"

Did she think him some sort of womanizer, always ready for a quickie? "No, Caro."

"Really?"

"I'm not celibate, if that's what you're asking. Haven't been since I lost my virginity at thirteen, and got a girlfriend at eighteen."

"You what? Oh, Kent, you're impossible!" Caroline laughed, the pained look in her eyes fading. "You must—"

"I'm particular who I sleep with."

"How particular?"

Heart hammering, he took her hand, and it was feminine, the kind made to skid along manly flesh. His gaze climbed to her just-right lips.... Cutting off fantasies before they got the better of him, he answered, "There's something very particular about you."

"You don't kiss like you're too particular. I'd say the fox has invaded the chick coop frequently."

"I'm well trained in henhouses." A chuckle rumbled his chest. "Actually, more like pigpens."

He regretted his comment, even before her exclamation. "Pigpens!"

"Just teasing." He preferred to keep details about the Corsican farm—where he'd learned the art of lovemaking—to himself. "I know quality, not quantity. I'm particular."

She wiggled a few inches in his opposite direction. "I am not going to sleep with you. I—"

"I didn't know you'd asked to 'sleep' with me. I thought you wanted itch relief for your leg. Of course, if 'sleep' is what you're after, I'm your man."

He angled toward her. Stretching each arm over the sweet being of her, and very aware of her soft, feminine flesh, he murmured, "Did you say you have an itch to scratch?"

"I wish you wouldn't do this. You make it hard for me."

"You got that right," he growled.

"You never quit. I've been smelling your scent on this pillow ever since I went to bed. You planned it that way, didn't you?"

"Lawyers never go to court without planning the attack," he said and cringed at how unprepared he was. Another something hit him. Political sensitivities—hell, plain old decency—warned that it wasn't nice to seduce a vulnerable woman.

Reluctantly he bent wires. "Caro, something hard and pointed is coming at you."

He wielded wire. Soon, Kent vowed silently, he would wield heated steel.

Chapter Five

There nights went by before Natalie slept without crying out for the someone who had never been there for her. Her sister spent each of those nights calming her, the days being spent learning how to bring smiles to a small face. The much-too-sexy male houseguest, an ace at scratching a woman's itches, showed her how. The two were enough to drive Caroline crazy.

Was it love?

It had to be more than mere interest, certainly more than Caroline's past involvement with the waifs at the Pasadena shelter. Her feelings bordered on those she'd felt for Frank's daughter, at least where Natalie was concerned.

Despite her misgivings about Kent, he forever steered Caroline to his positives. She was way too susceptible, when it came to him.

From her wheelchair, she gazed beyond a sunbath-

ing Greezy and across the backyard to the infant swing
Kent had hung from the branches of a live oak. It went
without recounting that installation hadn't begun well,
but careful instructions from a wheelchair-bound
coach had helped him along.

He now stood behind Baby, pushing the swing, receiving squeals of delight. His attentiveness moved
Caroline. It would be difficult, letting those two go,
but go, they must. Or did they have to? Of course they
did. Didn't they?

In the past Caroline gave up people who mattered
to her, usually against her will. She could do it again.
With the exception of Ruth, she'd learned to accept,
then carry on. This might feel like the beginnings of
love, these pings and pangs she had for Natalie and
Kent, but she had to face reality.

Sometimes love lost out.

How easy would it be, letting go this time? Playing
house, when she wasn't crunching numbers or day-
dreaming about a possible promotion, had given her a
taste of what she'd searched for with Frank, a home
life with a sensitive man and a baby to round out the
picture. But this was a temporary arrangement.

She had the urge to cry, not only for herself. *Baby's
too young to lose love. She's already lost her parents,
lousy though they were.*

Kent quit with the swing to carry Natalie to the
sandbox purchased yesterday. While the tyke happily
dug fingers into soft sand, he meandered over to Caroline. His fingers stuffed into back pockets of his sa-
fari shorts, he said, "All modesty aside, I think we're
doing good by her."

"I think so, too."

"What's it called?" he asked in the distinct way

used by two people who shared a bond and didn't need to clarify a question.

"Tools." She knew he meant the child-psychology manual they had pored over. "Tools to quiet night terrors."

"Ah, yes." He lifted his eyes, also remembering instructions on a combination of comfort, calm, a drink of water, a storybook and a night light.

"Doesn't the light bother you?" she asked.

Kent was now smiling down at her. Smiling that wonderful grin, made even more attractive by his sexy mustache; the smile went straight to her solar plexus.

"Your couch bothers me," he answered. "The light is nothing. But my feet are still asleep when I wake up."

She assessed his lofty form. "You're too tall."

"Too tall for what?" he countered and looped an arm around her neck to give her a whiff of her favorite scent.

She also got a reminder of his gigabyte of male appeal. She wrinkled her nose, loving their banter. "You're too tall for my sofa, that's what."

His face near hers, he winked. "At least I can sing."

"You do have a nice voice."

"Lullabies are easy. By the way, your singing voice has improved."

"That songbook you got at the bookstore helped," Caroline replied, shamed at her lack of singing ability.

"Yep." He scratched her nape lightly. "Can't say heavy metal carries much melody."

"Oh, you! Stop teasing."

"I'd rather tease you than eat. Unless *you're* the meal."

More than once he'd kissed her in the dark, after they had calmed Baby. A delicious shiver went through Caroline even now. Yet it was Kent who'd had the wherewithal to stop at kisses.

Caroline had wanted more—still did. It wasn't easy, trying to keep her mind on work and her possible promotion, when sexual urges wreaked havoc on her. Thank goodness *he* had more willpower than she. How or why he did, she didn't know and was too much a coward to explore.

Gathering her own wherewithal, she goaded, "Goody for you, you can sing. Too bad about the sofa. Never let it be said you don't suffer for four hundred an hour."

"Zero times zero is still zero, Ms. Statistician. I haven't billed a dime to Gnat Nat. And won't."

Caroline should have been shocked. Oddly, she wasn't. He might make the sounds of the avaricious, but his deeds told their own story. No one could give like Kent gave, unless they were made of top-grade stuff. "You're serious."

"It does me good to buy Gnat Nat the things a kid needs."

Was he speaking of his own childhood? Caroline tried to imagine his upbringing, but couldn't. Even though her mother was a washout, she'd had a father. What they had shared was special. Her toys may have been homemade, but at least she'd had them.

"You buy the toys you never had," she said, heart in her words.

Kent shrugged, squinting at the sun. "Right. Like I never had."

This hunk had the proverbial heart of gold, a heart with scars on it. He appealed to the woman in Caroline on so many planes. "You're awfully good to Baby. And to me."

He stepped behind the wheelchair to lay fingers on her shoulders. Kneading with eminent finesse, he massaged her muscles. Her tension disconnected, replaced by a certain euphoria. No, it wasn't merely from his touch. It was Kent the man who made her feel as if she were floating, and for the first time, she realized her great fortune, Kent Mackay coming into her life, for however long the stay.

"You can buy all the toys you like now," she commented. "You've earned that right. But it doesn't make up for the lost ones, does it?"

"No."

"Kent...how did you shake off your upbringing?"

"What makes you think I have?"

A question formed. Should she dare ask it? "Do you ever wonder what happened to your parents?"

"I know where they are." His fingers stilled. "They're like Gnat Nat's egg donor. Disinterested. I'd rather not discuss them."

Caroline nodded. "I understand."

And she did. Some things were too hard to talk about. She elected to consider the progressive. "I think you like doing for me, too. What can I give in return?"

His lips touched her ear, his mustache tickling the shell of it, drawing a quiver, before he answered, "I've always wanted to play doctor. You interested, little girl?"

"You beast." Her giggles almost drowned her words. "Doctor. The very idea!" Caught up in the giggles, she reached back to thump his collarbone. "Be serious!"

"Okay. I was teasing. But...you get the picture."

Where would they end up? Probably in bed. That wasn't a loathsome idea, although she did worry about the logic of becoming sexually involved with a temporary lover.

"'O! Me!'"

Her attention called away by Natalie's voice, Caroline smiled. Angel Baby had been calling her "'O'" for the past day or so, an endearing name, since it was hers alone.

Baby started to run toward them, but tripped and did a clumsy somersault that disturbed and irked the high-and-mighty Greezy.

The toddler's cries took Kent to the rescue, and the landlocked Caroline sat frustrated at her inability to move, yet it gave the opportunity for further exploration of her feelings.

She'd been panting over Kent in her heart, so what would be wrong with behaving like a nineties woman? Training, for one. Her father reared her not to give in to "pawing" males who wanted milk, not the cow. Thus, her experiences with sex had been marital. And not too hot.

Here she was, over thirty. She'd done her time in the marriage go-round. Shouldn't her newly earned freedom spill into every facet of her life? Yes.

But the next time she knew a man in every sense she wanted hot passion in bed with him. Feelings that went beyond lust would be an added plus. Kent's actions promised those things.

She might love Kent Mackay. How could she know for certain? Love, of course, could complicate matters. These considerations were as serious as supporting his ragged heart.

Eager not to cogitate her dilemma, Caroline considered Natalie, a sure avenue to take her mind from Kent.

What am I going to do about Baby? Not only must Kent's feelings be considered, so must the little one's. Plump, precious Baby, again playing in the sand, sought an audience of loved ones, as if she hadn't a care in the world.

"Kent, I'm worried about Baby. We should take her to a doctor. Those night terrors can't be good for her heart."

"She didn't have one last night. Besides, I've made an appointment with her Dallas pediatrician. It's about the same time you get your cast off."

"Should you wait that long?"

"The doc's a busy woman. Besides, you're in no condition to travel. I won't leave you here alone."

Caroline wouldn't argue. It seemed the longer she had this cast, the more worrisome it became. "You're planning to stay till I'm on my feet?"

"It's in Gnat Nat's best interest."

"Whose best interest? You're putting my well-being before hers."

His lips whitened beneath the mustache. "Caro, she's doing fine. Her condition isn't as serious as—"

"You always say that," Caroline broke in. "You're simply trying to make me feel better about Baby. Doesn't work. You must consider your client. She can't speak for herself."

"I am considering Natalie. Our being here is good for her." He crouched down and broke a blade of grass to twist between his fingers. "I'd like to stay until you're free of fiberglass. If that's agreeable with you."

She agreed, except for the pediatrician part. It *had* done Natalie good, receiving attention. Some things were as important as doctors. "Please stay."

"Yes!" One male fist went skyward in triumph. He was on his feet in a nanosecond, his arms around Caroline in another.

It started as a kiss of success, not unlike one would give to a friend at a happy moment. But it moved beyond friendship. Moved to heating passion.

Her wrists darted and crossed behind his neck, her breasts tingling as they abraded his chest. His lips became softer yet insistent, his upper lip brushing hers. When he mated their tongues, she welcomed it.

Yet he eased away. His eyes heavy with the undeniable passion that bowed between them, he whispered, "Thank you."

It took collecting wherewithal to say, "For a two-week stay? No need for that. I enjoy having Natalie here."

He ran fingers along her bare leg, rousing the same excitement elicited at each of his touches. The neglected little boy in him asked, "What about me?"

"It makes you late fixing our lunch," she tossed out.

"Kent Mackay, household drudge." He grinned. "That's me. I live to serve, aim to please."

"Go fix lunch, mister," she demanded as he started to kiss her again.

He clipped a salute, collected Natalie from the sandbox and headed into the house, leaving Caroline with cat company.

What a day. Kent set Natalie to her feet, then pulled out a kitchen chair and plopped down to rub his eyes with a thumb and forefinger. He and Natalie were making headway with Big Sister—a good thing. But, if Caroline were right about the pediatrician, then he'd gambled too freely on an emergency doctor's diagnosis.

He reached for the phone, punched in a series of digits before adding his calling-card number. When the party answered, he demanded, "Put Dr. McBride on the telephone."

Five minutes later he replaced the receiver in its cradle. And exhaled in relief. Jeanne McBride, after reading Natalie's most recent report, had assured him, "Everything looks fine. It won't hurt, waiting a few weeks for our appointment."

He walked to the back window, staring out. A shaft of sunlight glancing off a wheel of Caroline's chair, she watched a gamboling Greezy. The cat twirled, chasing a butterfly.

Up to now, Kent had tried to tell Caroline the whole truth about Natalie; she always jumped to conclusions. Maybe it was better this way. Her growing feelings for Baby Sister was his only firm hold, beyond sexual attraction.

"If I tell the truth," he said to Natalie, who pulled pans from a cabinet, "I'll lose the case before it gets to jury."

Kent wouldn't lose. He'd prepared himself...in every discreet way. If it looked like he might begin to lose, then why not filibuster?

Caroline took a glance at the kitchen window; Kent stood behind it. He waved, then stepped back. Dear Kent.

Suddenly something flew through the air. Greezy.

She cleared the wheelchair and almost clawed a monarch. Landed, she made another pass at her quarry, then retreated behind a bush, evidently thinking the butterfly wouldn't see her.

"Crazy cat. You don't fool anybody. And who am I fooling?" Caroline swallowed, recalling Kent's kisses and thinking about a young orphan. "You're not enough for me. Neither is work. I want more."

At the very least, she ought to provide a home for Natalie. Visions of Kent formed in the picture. Giving, tender Kent. What would it be like, having more children in the group?

Her feelings for him weren't set in her mind, much less in her heart, and they hadn't even played doctor, yet here she was, imagining picket fences. Only vaguely had she thought about a place called Fill-Er-Fast.

Greezy suddenly abandoned the butterfly romp. Hopping onto Caroline's lap, she purred up into her face.

"Cat, I'm new to a job, new to my profession and new to taking care of a baby. If this promotion comes through, how can I be Super Sister? What would I do with Natalie when I'm on the road? Hire another au pair? Find a day-care center? I don't know where to start. I know, I know. Many women make great single mothers, and their prospects aren't nearly as good as mine, but they ease into the job. I don't know how to be a sister, much less a protector. She needs a *mother*."

What sort of scars would Natalie carry into adulthood?

Greezy, unusually attentive, began to knead Caroline's breasts. "Murr-ow?"

"To tell the truth, sweetie, I'm not sure I can handle being tied down, depending on outsiders and worrying about a sickly baby who might end up a head case. Lord, if I don't sound just like Ruth."

That analogy struck Caroline. Hit her like a two-by-four between the eyes. "I am Ruth. Ruth all over again."

Tears streamed down her cheeks.

Greezy tried to lick them away, but Caroline didn't want sympathy. A spade of self-loathing went through her. *I'm just like Ruth, just like Ruth.*

Something was wrong with Caroline, and had been since before lunch. She worried Kent. In her usual manner, she tuned him out, refusing to discuss the problem. Had she somehow found out about his call to Jeanne McBride, M.D.? Paranoid, that thought. If Caroline knew, she'd lash out at him.

For the next couple days she continued to behave strangely, although she didn't refuse the child and made more care-and-comfort efforts. Caroline even got good at changing diapers.

But she wasn't herself.

"Kent, what if Baby soils her britches, here at the zoo?"

That was where they were, on the third day after the light had gone out of Caroline's eyes. The famed Brackenridge Zoo was surprisingly empty this August morning.

She had Natalie in her lap, Kent pushing the wheel-chair up the incline from the ticket cage, toward the elephants. He was beginning to think his instincts were all wrong.

He answered, "If we need to change her, we do it."

"Where?" She stared up at him, tenseness around her mouth. "I could wheel her into the ladies' room, but—"

"Caro, you worry too much," cautioned the arch-worrier.

"She's heavy," Caroline groused as they passed the big cats and the koalas. "You hold her awhile."

"Won't hurt her to walk for a few minutes." Once he put Natalie on the ground, and firmly held her hand in his, he said to her sister, "I'll take her to the aviary. Will you be okay here?"

"I won't. It's hot. My head is frying. Oh, never mind. I'll wheel to the seal show. Won't burn up there."

"You're mighty testy today," he commented, while Caroline took off.

"So what!"

He glanced around, glad no one else heard their "domestic" argument. He whipped Natalie into his arms, and loped after Caroline. "What's wrong with you?"

Not a syllable met his question. She braked the chair at the top of the open-air arena, where the marine show had begun. Natalie squealed in delight at the clever exhibition. Leaning on a limestone retaining wall, Kent placed her on his lap to let her get a good look at the seals and their straight men.

He cast a sidelong glance at Caroline. Her eyes were on the show, but enjoy it she didn't. She sat glumly.

"I thought this outing would be good for you," he said.

"It's hot. I'm tired. My leg aches."

She looked miserable. Clumps of hair had escaped her ponytail. Perspiration made her blouse adhere to her skin, the outline of a serviceable white bra visible against it. This was no time for lascivious thoughts, yet Kent gawked at a wealth of feminine breasts. How would they feel in his hands?

"Why don't I take off my blouse so you can get a better look?" she asked sourly.

He jacked up his eyes. "Would you like a soda?"

"No."

"How about a kiss?" He frowned, exasperated. "A shot of vodka? A vial of strychnine?"

"Hush up. I'm watching the seals."

Natalie took that moment to get restless. She squirmed off Kent's lap, then toddled over to the wheelchair. "'O?"

Caroline bent her head downward, her line of sight stopping on the pixieish girl in striped play clothes and leather sandals. Natalie gazed up at her, smiling and showing teeth.

That was when Big Sister broke into tears.

Kent went into action, getting his women out of the zoo. Fast. Once they were in the Cherokee, the air conditioner on high, and had driven onto Mulberry Drive, he asked, "What's up with you?"

"I told you. I'm tired and my leg is giving fits."

"You work too hard, impressing Fuzznuts Wanek."

"That is a nasty thing to call my employer."

"Not as bad as what I heard you rumbling this morning, when Fuzznuts called. I won't repeat it." One wrist on the steering wheel, Kent cocked a thumb toward the rear seat. "Little ears, you know."

Caroline surprised him, saying, "Baby deserves better than me."

By some stroke of luck they were now approaching one of San Antonio's curb-service restaurants. He wheeled in, then punched a button and barked into the speaker, "Two beers, three barbecue sandwiches and a glass of milk."

"Kind of early to be drinking, isn't it?" Caroline said.

"If you're talking Gnat Nat's just deserts, no time is too early."

"I don't like beer."

"Then drink milk! I'll pour your beer into her bottle. *She* could use a drink, if she knew what was going on here."

"She doesn't have any business eating barbecue, either." A shaking hand extended to pat the rosy little cheek. "If you think I'm going to let him get boozed up, Angel Baby, then drive on public roads, think again. You deserve all the best."

He gritted his teeth before jabbing a forefinger into the speaker button again. "Change those beers to limeades."

"You want cherries in them ades, sir?"

"Just send the damn drinks!"

His anger caused Natalie to cry. The order had arrived, the limeades half melted, before he and Caroline could shush her tears. It helped splitting a sandwich into fourths and giving her a portion. The smear of barbecue sauce did wonders.

Caroline poured milk into a baby bottle, then gave it into willing hands. "This is no way to treat a baby."

"Okay, we're not perfect," he said evenly, "giving a kid a barbecue sandwich and getting her upset. But we're doing our best. Counts for something. What more does a kid deserve?"

"Better than Ruth Perry."

"No disrespect to the dead, but she's gone. And will be forgotten."

"No." Caroline shook her head. "It's been said that a dark day arrives when a woman looks in the mirror and sees her mother. I've had my dark day. I am Ruth."

It stunned him, hearing that. "Let's go home. Natalie doesn't need to hear where this conversation is leading."

Kent backed out of the drive-in and headed straight for the duplex.

"Baby's asleep," Caroline announced, after having successfully cleaned up Natalie and cajoled her into a midday nap.

His back to Caroline, Kent stood with his hands shoved into his rear pockets, staring out the front window.

"Kent...we've got to talk about Natalie's future."

"I'd prefer to discuss why you think you're Ruth."

Caroline studied her hands. They appeared white and cold despite summer, almost without life, like an old woman's. She felt old right now. If not elderly, at least drained. The more she thought about comparisons, the more she realized how similar she and her mother were.

It wasn't an easy thing to confide; several times she'd considered asking for Kent's ear, but hadn't. Not until that exchange in the Cherokee. Anyhow, he needed to know her mind-set. He was, after all, Natalie's attorney. But would he understand? "I'm selfish, like Ruth. I never recognized it until lately, but I am."

"Don't be ridiculous."

"Hear me out, then ask yourself how ridiculous it is."

He turned from the window, a lock of hair tumbling over a furrowed brow. His eyes held the aspect of concern, his lips having tightened in dread. Before she could stop herself, Caroline found Kent's concern endearing.

"I've turned into a clinging vine," she said. "I'm all the things I've hated. I'm just like Ruth."

"You're no more like her than summer is to winter."

"But I am. I've always depended on someone. My dad. Then my husband. Frank was thirty and settled, had a child, when I married him. For security." And for children, although Caroline refused to think about that. "I tried to cling to him. I—I suppose I was looking for a father, when he needed a blow-up doll who could do housework."

"You didn't love him?"

"I thought so, at first. As I matured, I realized it wasn't love we had between us. Yet we both stuck it out, even though we were day and night."

"Why?"

"Hope died hard with me. As for Frank, he was content. I was good at housework, and I made a decent sexual vessel, when he wanted one."

"Um, how decent?"

"Kent Mackay, pay attention!"

Abashed, he shrugged. "Sorry. Couldn't help asking."

"I suppose you have a right." They did have something going, however doomed it was. Or wasn't. "Let's just say it was quantity not quality."

"For you? Or for Frank?"

Frank could have sex without once placing a hand on her, outside the breast-grope foreplay. "To slake my own self-centered passions, I read up. Watched TV programs. I needed to know the hot spots, so I could interest Frank in satisfying me. But I never once asked what it would take to heat his hot spots."

Kent's fingertip grazed her earlobe, rousing a quiver that she didn't *need* at a time like this.

"Honey," he said, "if he needed to be asked, he didn't deserve you."

"Well, the least I could have done was ask if he wanted to tie me up or something. Or if he wanted to be tied up. Or if he'd prefer something else. I don't know. Maybe a paper sack for my head would have worked," she added, trying for a lighter note amid the embarrassment of her admissions.

The laugh that shook Kent might have shaken the rafters, so robust was it. "I do believe, Ms. Grant, you are a tigress."

Ruth had been like a feral cat, and the similarities kept Caroline solemn.

Reverting to the whys, she wanted off the subject of sex. "I should tell you about my stepdaughter. I loved Sheralinn and pampered her. But I didn't have to do it full-time. Being a part-time stepmother gave me the liberty for my own interests. Going to evening school, dreaming of better times to come. When it became obvious those better times wouldn't be forthcoming, I left. Then Filmore Wanek fulfilled my needs. He gave me a chance to prove myself. I take and take, but I never really give."

"You give a lot of yourself to Natalie."

"For now."

"You enjoy it. Now could become tomorrow, too."

"I'll bet that's what Ruth thought, when she got pregnant with me. Then with Natalie. She wanted babies for whatever reason. She got them. Once she did, what happened? She dropped me. She did the same to Natalie, going off to Africa. Leaving her sickly baby to an au pair. She can't be blamed for dying, of course, but what if she'd come home? She would've tired of Natalie, would have done no telling what. In the very least she would've ignored her."

"That's speculation on your part."

"I knew the woman. And I know myself. Kent, I want that promotion. Want it so badly I can smell it, taste it, feel it, hear it. I want it! And I fear I'll do the same thing with Natalie—" *and with you* "—that Ruth did to me and Baby."

"I doubt that. You have Gnat Nat's money behind you. You needn't worry about hiring adequate help. Do your own thing, and give her what she needs."

Most women would kill for such an offer, and it even sounded good to Caroline, yet she shook her head. "You're not getting it, Kent. No amount of money, no amount of help, gives inner peace. Or the ability to make sacrifices of the heart."

"It won't be a sacrifice, giving her up now?"

Yes, it would. Of course it would. "I'm doing this for Natalie. I'm saying I *won't* fob another Ruth off on anyone, especially not on my sweet little sister. She deserves better."

"You're selling yourself short."

"As long as we're falling to clichés, don't forget, 'blood tells.'"

His jaw twitched. A muscle ticked in his right eye. His shoulders hunched slightly as he advanced on Caroline, and he might have frightened her, if she hadn't known his tenderhearted spirit, despite his occasionally shouted "damn."

He halted in front of her, clamped his fingers around the armrests of her chair. Leaning down, his gaze level with hers, he said, "You are not your mother. You're a fighter. Ruth was weak. You aren't. You never abandoned anyone in your life, except for that sorry-assed ex-husband of yours. You were an excellent daughter, seeing your father through his last illness. You must have been an excellent stepmother. And I don't want to hear any pap about how much you get from that buffoon boss of yours. He'll wring the life out of you, Caro. You just don't see it."

"Leave Filmore out of this."

Kent said, "Look at you. A cast up to your thigh, your shin and knee broken, just like your spirit. You know, if Ruth Perry were standing in this living room right now, I'd shake her till her teeth rattled for undermining your faith."

"You're one to talk. You're as messed up as I am."

"You could change all that."

Her eyes widened.

"No comment, Caro?"

"I am Ruth."

He tapped her jaw lightly. "I stand corrected. It's *you* who needs her teeth rattled."

"You lay one hand on me, Mackay, and I'll have you up on beating charges."

"No, sweetheart. It's called 'assault and battery.'"

"Don't be so doggone superior."

"Why shouldn't I? I've got faith in you, Caro. I think you can go the distance. I know you love that kid sleeping in the next room. And I know—"

"You know nothing," she denied.

"I know you need to be—"

"Why don't you just hush?"

Kent didn't. "You need love."

Tension continued to zap between them; it heated her insides. Her feelings had nothing to do with Natalie or Ruth, and certainly not with the future. They had everything to do with sexual longing. Hang the circumstances that had brought her to this moment in time. Hang the future.

But would he do as before, and demonstrate more of his excellent kissing? If he did, Caroline feared the worst. That she'd go after him, even if it meant getting on crutches.

Or crawling.

Why?

She loved Kent Mackay.

In her own selfish, needy way, Caroline loved him. For now.

Her hand wrapped a portion of his rear. "Would you like for me to tie you up? Or something?"

Chapter Six

Her desperate means weren't necessary.

Bedroom eyes hot with desire, Kent slipped a fingertip up her arm to trace her lips. "You don't need whips or chains to turn me on. Just the sight of you does it. I may be a heel and a rogue, but I ache for you. Cast or no cast. Shall we…?"

Selfishly, Caroline wouldn't argue, not with the promise he presented. "It's only a cast."

He snaked an arm beneath her legs, the other behind her back. Oh, he did smell good. In a split second he held her aloft and was carrying her to the sofa, where he deposited her, as if she were a china doll.

Like a drug, he drew her into his being, masterfully, wholly. This was wild, crazy, magic at the very least. His sandalwood aura, mixed so wondrously with the unique scent of Kent, captured her and held fast. She saw his eyelids close. She heard a murmur, her pet name. And then he angled toward her. At first his palms slipped along her ribs, then his right hand was between her shoulder blades, his hips near hers.

He was growing hard. Very hard.

That was when she caught her breath.

"Caro," he groaned and welded his mouth to hers.

Suddenly, neither could get enough of the other. Their tongues twined, their bodies bowed and pressed, as much as they could, considering the cast. She wanted him, yearned to know the mysteries of this man; her body gave full approval.

His lips left hers, trailing to the space between her nose and eyes. He coasted over a closed eyelid, then meandered to her cheek. It was sensual mincemeat he made of her ear, alternately puffing streams of breath into it, then laving it.

"What does it take to turn you on?" he whispered.

"Exactly what you're doing."

"Good."

His sensual assault persisted. One hand trailed to her breast, burnishing the underside of it. Then he eased her bra over the hillock...and twisted downward to make a circular motion with his tongue, while his manhood nudged rhythmically against her pelvis, despite the fiberglass cast.

Her fingers sliced into his hair, her nails digging, as he drew into his mouth the crest that ached for him. Where she had been moist for him now was even more so.

With her ex-husband, sex had never been this exciting.

Mindless desire, infinite curiosity, drove her to say, "Want to feel it."

He allowed her plea. He helped her dig into the top

button of his chinos, and didn't object as she went beneath his steel-hard manhood, then surrounded it. He did growl as she did the latter.

"You're very large," she whispered.

"Say you don't mind."

"Mind? Every self-seeking vein in my body is thrilled."

Eyes half-shuttered, he stroked her cheek. "Don't ever forget. You are Caro. Only Caro. And I want you just the way you are."

This, naturally, was the wrong thing to say, since it further reminded her of the obvious. Her maternal stock ran rampant. She was taking from a man who needed to receive.

Refusing to trap him in a Ruth-like web, she shoved his shoulder. "Get up before I do assault and battery on you."

For a moment he gawked, astounded. He let out a breath and shook his head. Buttoning his trousers, he muttered, "At least you're getting the vernacular right."

It hurt to watch him stand and stalk away, not comprehending what had turned her from him. But didn't he know? Hadn't she made herself clear, before he had carried her to the sofa?

Damn, why did life have to be so complicated?

Desire still fighting for attention, she straightened her clothes and angled to sit up. She took a calming breath. For him, for Natalie, they needed clarity and plans.

"Let's talk law," she said.

"Law?" Kent wheeled her chair to the sofa. "You want to talk law, when we've just crawled all over each other?"

She nodded. "I want you to *act*. Break Don Perry's will. Find adoptive parents for Natalie."

She expected an argument.

Her mouth dropped when he replied, "All right, I'll do it. Thanks for the kisses and hugs, honey. I'd better pack. It's a long drive to Dallas. I want to be home before it gets too late. I'll need rest—Gnat Nat will, too—before we face the CPS folks tomorrow."

He'd leave? Now? Wasn't this what she asked for? Finally he'd do as suggested, yet it had a hollow feel to it.

Without another word he collected his stuff and Baby's. Caroline got into her chair and backwheeled into the kitchen. Returned to the living room. By the time he had the high chair and his suitcase to his car, she began to perspire. He got the first load of clothes into the Cherokee, and she grew frantic.

Caroline was waiting at the front door, when he trudged up the walk for the last load, his head lowered, the afternoon sun highlighting a dark head and broad shoulders. *I love him. I love that baby. If I let them go, I'll never get them back.*

She went for self-preservation. "I'm not a quarter perfect. Natalie deserves better than me, but I'll do my best for her. I want to be her sister forever."

His head lifted slowly. The sun that had shone on his black hair and manly shoulders wasn't nearly as bright as his smile. "Thank you, Caro" was all he said.

"Kent, shall we celebrate?"

He glanced across the table at the River Walk café to Lorraine Hardwicke. Behind her was a set of stairs leading up and over a canal, greenery growing on the limestone railing.

Lori Hardwicke looked sensational in any background. At thirty-three, she exuded confidence, from her sleek fair hair to perfectly tailored designer clothes to the dauntlessness that came from being born beautiful, smart and heir to Dallas's most-successful law firm.

Once he'd telephoned to report Caroline agreed on Natalie's behalf, this noted criminal-defense attorney had told him, "I have good news, too. My client walked." She thereafter suggested lunch and hopped the first plane out of Love Field.

"Well, Kent?" she said, smiling at Natalie, who perched in a high chair, facing the river.

"No celebrations."

He had celebrated with Caroline and Natalie last night, a party that ended with him on the sofa and the bedroom door closed between one alluring woman and a frustrated man. Despite her surrender with regard to her little sister, there would be no seducing the golden-haired lady who hadn't gotten past Ruth deserting her.

"When do you plan to return to Dallas?" Lori asked.

"The end of next week. Caro will be on her feet by then."

The waiter interrupted by flourishing salads. Kent cut Natalie's into small bites and left her be to eat it, which she preferred. Thankfully, Caroline had remembered to include a bib in the diaper bag. She was great at details.

Lori didn't eat. "It's not like you to shift your caseload. With you out of pocket like this, billings are down. I want my best money-maker in the office.

Come home, Kent. Besides, I'm bored, not having my pal to chat with.''

They were pals, and had been for a long while. More than once, he and Lori had been there for each other.

"Try to buck up," he teased, and grinned. "I won't be gone much longer. I don't want to leave Caro, not till the doctor releases her. We've got to work out details for Natalie's day care, too."

"Oh?"

"I'm here for Gnat Nat's sake." Voicing his mind-set helped rectify it. "I owe it to Don's memory. We were friends, you know. Beyond doing the right thing by his daughter, she's my duty. Besides, I'm long overdue for a vacation."

"Okay, all right. I'm convinced. Let me know if there's anything I can do to help you."

It wasn't Lori's help he needed. If Kent had his ifs, he'd cajole Caroline into a trip to Dallas before the probate-court hearing. Not an easy task. She intended to be in Fill-Er-Fast's offices as soon as a certain fiberglass anchor became flotsam.

Yet he wanted her with him. Just the three of them—Caroline, Natalie, Kent. One for all, all for one. The Three Musketeers. Their relationship had been a whirlwind one, yet he knew in his heart that Caroline was the one for him.

How fair would it be, though, asking her to change her dreams?

A couple then caught Kent's eye. They passed on his right, the middle-aged woman pushing a young man's wheelchair.

"Oh, dear," said the lady, "another set of stairs."

"Turn me 'round, Mother. We'll go back the way we came."

"Doug, you wanted to see the starving-artist show."

Frustration emitted from eyes that ought to be too young to know infirmity. "Just turn me 'round."

"Waiter!" Kent called out, his plea answered in a flash. "Let's get this fellow up these stairs and down the ones across the canal. Lori, keep an eye on Gnat Nat."

The mother beamed. "Oh, thank you, gentlemen."

Her son saved gratitude until reaching the bottom of the far stairs, yet the chagrin of dependence dulled his features.

Kent merely clipped a salute and gave the helpful waiter a meaningful glance; they retook the stairs. Kent went back to Natalie and Lori.

The lady lawyer was holding a glass of milk to Natalie's lips. She said to Kent, "That was decent of you. But you're the sort of fellow to be a Boy Scout."

"Being around Caro gave me a new understanding for how tough it must be, being physically challenged."

"Don't get too keen on playing Boy Scout. It might cause a conflict of interest. I had more than a celebration in mind, coming here today." A French-manicured finger fiddled with a choker of pearls. "Lew Chambliss is going ahead with his suit against Snappy Sours."

Chambliss, a quadriplegic, had been threatening to sue Kent's client over a lack of handicapped parking spaces at the Snappy Sours headquarters. When Kent left Dallas, that was all it had been—a threat. This could sabotage his plans for his campaign to win Caroline.

"I'll get my staff on the horn," he said. "If they can't take care of the preliminaries, I'll make a trip to Dallas."

"Kent Mackay, you say that as if you'd sooner have a root canal. You really must have it bad for Caroline Grant. I hope she's worthy of you. I'd hate to see you hurt again, like you were over that redhead who did you wrong."

The redhead was very much past history. But he appreciated Lori's concern. Never having had a sister, he couldn't objectively equate what it must be like to have one, but to his way of thinking, Lori made a great surrogate sister.

"I hope I don't get burned," he allowed in reply.

"I hope you don't, either. Kent—"

"Kenn..." Natalie smiled, then tossed a cracker.

"She's a spirited little thing," Lori commented without rancor.

"She is. I hope never to break that spirit. I'd like to see her spoiled silly."

"Guess you want to take back that statement you made one night. You remember. When you said you'd sooner raise orchids than kids."

"Caro's not interested in raising kids. If we work things out, we'll have our family already—Gnat Nat."

"Kent, no! Please tell me you love this woman enough to take a chance on—"

"Lori," he cut in, stringing her name out. "Don't."

She eased up on sisterly advice. "You've been looking for Ms. Right. I'm glad you found her. When can we meet?"

"Soon."

She reached to pat his forearm. "I wish you well."

He ate in silence, giving his attentions to Natalie and listening to Lori move on to law matters. Yet having her blessing was a relief.

Her blessing, however, was premature, as were his ideas about the Three Musketeers. Caroline might have capitulated on Natalie, but she hadn't said a word about him. Her career still ranked number one. And Ruth Perry continued to haunt her. What could he do to brighten their prospects?

They weren't completely unappealing, her prospects.

The strangest thing had happened since Caroline agreed to take custody of Natalie. She became a tiny bit more confident about being a sister. If not confident, then at least less frightened. Kent helped her along, naturally.

She didn't regret loving him. And love him, she did. What was love, if not for lust mixed with respect, mixed with the determination to do what was best for the loved one? Did he love her? Where was his fire? She needed it. Yet he hadn't made another move. Why?

And what had he meant, making that remark about changing things for him?

She dared not ask.

Right now, the afternoon before she had an appointment with her orthopedic specialist, Caroline would finish trimming Baby's fingernails. "Sit still," she said softly but firmly. "I don't want to cut you."

Natalie paid no mind. She squirmed. She fidgeted. She complained in her toddler way.

"Want some sherbet?" Kent cajoled from across the room.

That got Baby's attention. Caroline's, too. Darn him, he was spoiling this child silly. But didn't children need a spoiling influence to offset nail trimmings and the serious facets of being reared?

Caroline would lend the seriousness. For now, forever.

"Sit still, Natalie Perry," she admonished gently. "Then we'll have sherbet."

Amazing what a bribe could do. Those fingernails looked great in no time. Kent got the dish of dessert, then tried to situate Baby in her high chair. Trouble was, she objected. Natalie could be quite vocal with objections.

In no time Angel Baby was bent over the coffee table, her behind swaying from side to side. She smeared sherbet into her hair, her clothes and everything else within reach.

"She really is cute," Caroline commented with familial pride, despite several levels of dismay.

"That she is," he said, his gaze on Caroline.

"I'm worried."

"What now, Caro?"

"We didn't get any good nanny candidates from our newspaper advertisement."

"Too bad we're not in Dallas. My cleaning lady was delighted to have Gnat Nat around the house."

A melancholy feeling seeped through Caroline. He was leaving San Antonio, once she was out of this cast and they had hired someone to take care of Natalie. Naturally, she'd travel to Dallas for the probate hearing, despite the time it would take from work, but how would she manage?

What would Ruth have done?

What a laugh.

Ruth wouldn't be fighting for anyone.

Like Kent had assured her, Caroline wasn't so much her mother's daughter after all.

He said, "I'd bet good money Angie Cortez would jump at the idea of taking care of Natalie while you work. She's a great housekeeper, and has six kids of her own."

"If she's a housekeeper with a family to go home to at night, I doubt she'd have energy for a rambunctious toddler."

"Rhetorical. Angie's in Dallas. Fill-Er-Fast is here."

Caroline started to imagine what the inside of Kent's Dallas house looked like, but Greezy jumped on the coffee table; Natalie offered a spoonful of orange sherbet.

"Scat, pest!" Caroline shoved chair wheels, eating up the distance between herself, a too-generous little girl and a cat who had a yen for any sort of nourishment.

Kent beat her to the table. "Shoo!"

The tortie, hissing at the interloper male, retaliated by giving him a left hook to his wrist, several quick ones, before she flounced off, seriously insulted.

Sad blue eyes lifted to the adults. "Kit cat...?"

"Do not share your food with Greezy." Caroline wiggled at the hips to reach for her sister. Once Natalie was in her lap, she advised, "Kitty has her own food."

Those babyish eyes widened, as if her mind went to devious paths, toward helping herself to *Greezy's* food.

Kent disappeared to the kitchen, showing up with

another bowl of sherbet, which provoked Caroline to say, "Oh, no. She's had enough. Get her colors."

Crayons and sheets of paper didn't hold much attraction for Natalie. She made two green marks on what had been a draft of a report to Fill-Er-Fast, then twisted in restlessness. Looking first at Kent, then at Caroline, she said, "'Ay?"

That meant play, as in outside in her sandbox.

As usual, Kent sprang into action, carrying each sister in turn down the back steps. Natalie ran to sand and shovels. Kent helped Caroline to the picnic table.

Seated on the bench, she watched Natalie, both with love and pride. She adored that child and loved the man, too. How nice it would be to have a family with Kent. There. She'd admitted it, at least to herself.

Talk about jumping the gun!

Talk about being unfair, yet Caroline fantasized about tomorrows filled with richness of the heart. Idiocy, it was plain idiocy, even thinking about that. But what was wrong with fantasizing? Dreams had been her ticket to independence.

Kent neared the picnic table. "Penny for your thoughts."

"They'd cost you a million bucks. But I will say this. I'll be glad to get rid of this thing." Caroline thumped the cast. "Then I'm going to run circles and jump hoops. And cook us a fantastic dinner. And read the back issues of the tabloids."

Afterward I'm going to get serious about what's in your head and heart. If she was assuming too much, then she needed to know it, before her dreams got out of hand.

Studying one dreamboat of a man, she asked, "Any

chance you're turned on by dill salmon and parsley potatoes?''

Her meaning connected; he winked. "Works for me.''

"Fantastic!''

"You've never been so beautiful, so radiant,'' Kent observed in a sexy voice that rose like a promise in the dark. "But don't make too many plans. You'll want to ease into being Caroline Grant, dynamo.''

"Oh, pooh! I'm not listening to any naysaying. I like salmon. You do, too. And we both know Baby likes it.''

He groaned while chuckling, and he eased onto the picnic bench, close to Caroline. "She moves fast. Yesterday, I thought I could reach the Salmon Delight before she got to it.''

Caroline joined in laughter. "I hope you won't tell Judge Miller I allowed her close to a can of cat food. I promise to do better in the future. Anyhow, you're the one who was supposed to keep an eye on her.''

"That's hearsay, Ms. Grant. I will confide in the judge. I sure will.'' Rascal to the bone, Kent waggled closer to his prey. "Unless you give me a kiss.''

"That's blackmail,'' she answered, thrilled at the thought. Maybe a serious conversation could take place now, instead of after a dilled-salmon dinner.

"Yep, blackmail.'' Kent tilted Caroline's chin with the crook of his finger. His other hand clasped her shoulders and then his fingers trailed up and down her arm, elevating her pulse. "How 'bout that kiss, chick?''

He tasted like orange sherbet, sherbet warmed by desire's fire. At the moment she arched forward to deepen their embrace, he levered to stand. "Let's not wear you out."

"Kent!"

"Caro, I want to make love to you. But let's wait. Tomorrow, that cast will be gone. Then I'll love you. Me, Tarzan. You, Jane."

His was a wise suggestion. Tomorrow would dawn, and the evening held infinite promise, yet Caroline had done a lot of thinking lately. It was only fair to lay her cards on the table, before they got further involved.

Three times she set out to speak with him, and three times she lost her nerve. Playing her hand would take liquid fortification.

That evening, as he tickled Natalie's chin, Kent heard a terse "Put her to bed, please."

His favorite golden girl made for the kitchen; Kent readied Natalie for the night. Thankfully the child went right to sleep. He followed her sister's path, where she poured a tall glass of cola then splashed in a generous amount of Tennessee whiskey.

Except for one shared bottle of white Zinfandel, he'd never seen her take a drink. This was serious.

Caroline drank half the glass silently. Kent sat on a kitchen chair and watched, keeping just as mum. Mostly, he allowed himself an unfettered study. Every gesture she made, every movement of her hands or lips, each expression in her eyes, fascinated him. He was besotted at the sight of her, from the burnished beauty of her hair, to each womanly curve, to the toes that could use some nail polish. This was *the* woman.

"How do you feel about me?" she asked bluntly.

Her question took him aback. How should he answer? He loved her. A declaration, or any mention of the Three Musketeers, needed a lead-up, though. "I understand you."

"Think so?"

"I do. And I admire everything about you," he answered, going for the middle ground.

Giving her profile, she studied a blank spot on the wall. "What did you mean, that night after the zoo?" Her nose wheeled toward him. "I don't recall the exact wording, but you said something like, I can 'change things' for you."

"What are *you* saying, Caro?"

"I'll be at work in no time, as soon I—we—find someone to watch Baby. You can't ignore your law practice forever."

Even though he loved her, should he ask her to give up her ambition? He went for broke. "Come to Dallas with me. Find a new job. Let Angie take care of Gnat Nat. Seems simple enough."

"Come to Dallas with you?" Her tigress eyes rounded.

"Once we're there, we'll see what the future offers."

An eloquence of emotions swept across her oval face, before one brow arched. "Are you asking me to be your mistress?"

Not hardly. The urge to propose marriage welled. Go slow, he told himself and took her hand. He said softly, "I'm not going to ask anything until I know what goes with *you.*"

"I haven't been honest. I have no idea how honest you've been with me, although I have no reason to doubt you. But I will say this. You don't know me."

Shamed, he turned his gaze away. "I know a lot about you," he muttered.

"Do you really, Kent? I doubt it."

"You always sell yourself short, so I suppose yours is an ingress to something like that. Let's have it. Both barrels."

Her gaze loitered for what had to be an entire minute. "Do you know why I left Frank?"

"He was a Neanderthal who didn't want you to move ahead."

"Partly so. But that's not why I finally left. I learned something, something I couldn't live with. He lied. Lied by omission. I went into marriage, expecting children."

"Children?"

Her chin ducked; her fingers trembled. "When I didn't get pregnant, I wondered why."

"I—I thought you didn't want to bear children."

Gaze moving upward to his, she said, "That's where you don't know me."

Kent found a kitchen chair and sat down heavily. "What are you saying, Caro?"

"I didn't give up on marriage till I found out Frank couldn't have children. You see, he'd made certain of never having another." Her torment-laden voice struck Kent to the core, as she admitted, "He neglected to tell me he had a vasectomy *before* we got married."

That was when Kent poured his own shot of whiskey. Neat. He gulped the strong liquid, his brain ablaze. Where was she leading? he wondered, fearing the worst; any mention of begetting children left him too uncomfortable for words.

"Kent, I want children. I can't make them on my own."

His gaze settled on Caroline, and suddenly it hit him. He stared at a stranger. He'd assumed wrong about her. And there she sat, alluding to having babies with *him.*

"What's the matter, Kent?" A lovely hand went to the curve of her throat. "You look a little peaked."

Kent felt more than "peaked." Could he continue sitting upright? With more of a croak than he wished to convey, he said, "There's Fill-Er-Fast—"

"Many career women have families. Want to know my big secret, Kent? I've lied to myself over and over. I intend to have kids."

Plant your forearms on the table. Else you'll fall flat.

"Kent? Kent! Are you going to faint?"

Chapter Seven

"What's troubling you?"

Caroline glared at her doctor. "You tell me this cast may be replaced by another one, yet you ask such a question? Dr. Payne, you do live up to your name."

Joseph Payne wrote something on her chart, probably physician's shorthand for "what a bitch." Maybe she had it coming. She had been awful today. Who wouldn't be?

This was not a good day.

Kent had Natalie at the Children's Museum, having dropped Caroline at the door to this office suite, a terse "Call my cell phone when you're finished, and I'll pick you up" was his farewell.

He'd been that way since last night. But she had no time, not now, to chafe over the big goof.

The doctor said into his intercom, "Nurse, escort Ms. Grant to Room C."

Being wheeled down the hall to a room cluttered with assorted saws, plasters and splints, plus X-ray equipment, Caroline worried. Kent wouldn't like her going to work. Oh? Considering his offhandedness, he wouldn't mind. Last night, when she fretted he might pass out, she'd pegged his strange behavior on mixing alcohol with allergy medication. This morning could be blamed on a hangover.

What a screwball way to justify Kent Mackay.

Her big mouth, spewing secrets, had turned him off.

"Stay still, ma'am. I wouldn't want to cut you."

Caroline hadn't even realized she'd gotten on a flat table or that Nurse Armstrong had a circular saw poised over the cast. This should have been a happy moment.

When she got a gander at her leg for the first time since July fourth, she cringed. And it wasn't necessarily over bristly hairs and skin gone scaly and dry; any fool in her right mind would cringe at that. The big problem was, the muscles in her right leg had atrophied.

"We'll X-ray you here." The nurse moved behind a lead-glass partition. "Hold your breath. Don't move."

Caroline had no trouble obeying. She didn't feel much like breathing or moving. Why did nothing ever go smoothly?

I'll simply go to work. That's all I can do.

The doctor entered the room a few minutes later to turn a bright smile on her. "Don't scowl, Ms. Grant. I won't be putting another cast on your leg. It's fine!"

She heaved a sigh of relief.

But if Joseph Payne hadn't helped her down from the table, she would have fallen.

There was no way she could walk unaided.

There was no way she'd call on Kent for help. She simply couldn't face his coldness. Not now. She called a taxi.

At half past six that evening, Kent parked at the back entrance to the Fill-Er-Fast building. He glanced at Natalie, then craned his neck to peer inside a glass doorway. Five minutes ago, and a good six hours after he'd expected her summons, Caroline rang his cellular phone to say, "I'm finished for the day." Now, an aluminum walker preceding her, her hair knotted atop her head, she made her way toward the door. Her slow, pained way.

"It's showtime," he mumbled to Natalie, not looking forward to conversation.

Kent alighted from the four-wheeler, bounded around it and loped up two steps to the entrance. Like last night, he was caught surprised. Never before had they stood eye to eye. While she wasn't categorically short, she did seem small to Kent. Small and cuddly. And she wanted something he refused to provide.

He scowled, fingers bracing her upper arm. "Take it easy."

Her face turned up, and she nearly missed the step.

"Pay attention to what you're doing," he scolded, his meaning double.

"Yes. Of course."

Not wanting to talk, he got her into the passenger seat. They drove silently, even Natalie respecting the need for quiet.

As they neared the Monte Vista district, Caroline said, "Stop at H-E-B, and I'll run in and buy some salmon."

"Forget salmon. You've been 'running' all day."

They reached her duplex and got Natalie settled in the high chair with a plate of leftover chicken and rice before anything else got said. It was Caroline who spoke.

The walker against her thighs, she was peering into the refrigerator. "I swear we had some green beans in here."

"Natalie and I ate them at lunch."

Caroline turned her head so fast that a bobby pin came loose, a mass of hair tumbling to her shoulders. Kent liked it better loose, but said nothing as she refastened the knot.

"Kent, Baby needs vegetables."

"She ate two helpings at lunch. That should do her."

"I don't know. That baby book said, and you did, too—"

Kent didn't listen to the rest. He marched to the living room to grab the TV remote control and flopped into the overstuffed chair. A purple dinosaur sang and danced on the screen.

Greezy, having parked atop the TV previously, reared her head. "Murr-ow." She thereafter hopped onto Kent's knee. Stretching her neck, she raked her chin along his jaw.

"Ah-choo!" It was all he could do to grab a tissue. Shell-shocked and disoriented over Caroline's wish for kids, he'd forgotten to take his pill this morning. "Scat," he snarled.

It took a number of attempts to dislodge Greezy. Kent filed to the bathroom, got medication from his shaving kit and cupped his palm under the faucet for enough water to swallow the pill. He needed to get out of here. He couldn't take cat hair.

He couldn't take total honesty.

Yet Caroline needed it. Had all along. If he were candid with her, he'd settle past debts. That he'd known Natalie's heart condition was not as serious as he'd let on. That he didn't want kids of his own. That he didn't love Caroline enough to change his mind on the latter. It wasn't in him, that much love.

Just as Caroline hadn't wanted to fob another Ruth off on Natalie, Kent wouldn't hand his own blood to a new generation.

He was halfway down the front porch before he realized that he couldn't just leave. Caroline needed help. Natalie needed it. He couldn't turn his back. He didn't want to. Dammit, he loved those women. He just couldn't love himself.

Her heart heavy, her leg tired and sore, Caroline sang a lullaby as best she could to the baby in this crib. At last Natalie's eyes closed. Now to deal with why Kent had left.

Aided by the walker, Caroline passed the front window. Why, he wasn't gone. There was his nice white vehicle, parked where it ought to be. But where was he?

She found him. In the same jeans and cotton shirt he'd worn to pick her up from Fill-Er-Fast, he sat on the front porch, his head down, his wrists balanced on knees.

What could she say to him? "Are you hungry?"

"No."

She flipped the porch light on, even though dark had yet to fall. "I'm hungry."

"Call Dominick's. Have them send over an All The Way."

"I already have."

"Oh."

"May I sit down by you?" she asked.

He shoved to his feet, turning in the last rays of summer sunlight to assist her to a seat on the step. Momentarily she stared. Unaccustomed to looking at him from a standing position, she assessed the lofty height that gave him an aura of a gentle, protective titan.

Yet he'd never been this distant. The ravaged features went right to her heart without stopping until they reached her eyes, where tears threatened.

She sat down.

He retook a step and was sitting beside her, several inches between them, but not far enough to deny her a whiff of his cologne.

Should she mention last night? Should she try to put him at ease about it? No. To say anything would be as clever as striking a match near a gasoline pump.

"I know you're angry because I went straight to work today," she began, knowing this struck another volatile match, but one she could handle. "And didn't ask you for a ride."

"You got that right," he replied and scratched the chest hair revealed beneath the open collar of his shirt.

A small delivery van pulled onto the driveway, cutting conversation short. Kent stood, as if to dig for his wallet.

"Don't." She slid fingers into her skirt pocket. "My treat. Political sensitivities, you know."

"Women don't buy my food, PS or no PS."

"Don't be a fuddy-duddy," she said and offered bills.

Pizza box balanced in one hand, the delivery boy leered. "No one ever accused me of being old-fashioned. You wanna buy mine, lady? How 'bout Saturday night."

"Shove off." As Kent barked, he thrust greenbacks into the boy's fist and grabbed the pizza box. "Now."

The delivery van's motor revved; Caroline placed money on the step next to her, and grinned. His show of jealousy couldn't have come from an indifferent man. Maybe all wasn't lost.

Kent set the box atop the porch and scooped up her money. He positioned the walker away and hunched over her, their faces mere inches apart. Features stony, his eyes anything but, he shoved cash into her pocket...and his fingers lingered. She felt the circular motions he made on her hip; they spiraled through her entirety.

"Don't ever embarrass me like that again," he said with a growl and jerked his hand from her pocket.

"Again" was the key word, as Caroline assessed it.

"Get over it, Kent. Pizza, or who pays for it, isn't the problem." It might start an explosion, but she couldn't run scared forever. "About last night—"

"I won't discuss last night."

"I think we should. I started out simply to get into your mind. Apparently you don't want me there."

"I'm not ready for brain picking." He set the pizza box atop her legs and swung down to the step. "Let's eat."

She'd forgotten how bad Dominick's best was. No. The ingredients had nothing to do with her lack of appetite. A quick glance at Kent's profile assured her of his own lack of appetite. He hadn't even bitten into a slice.

Staring at his slice of All The Way, he sighed, then tossed the wedge to a dog who wandered up. The shaggy white mutt gobbled it in three bites before sitting on haunches to beg for more. The cur received Caroline's dinner for her troubles.

Once the pooch pranced to greener pastures, Kent glanced at Caroline, the porch light bathing each angle of his face. Surprisingly, he didn't form an argument.

"How did your afternoon go?"

"Actually, it went well. But I..." Caroline searched her memory for her earlier response, when she'd sat in a meeting with Filmore Wanek and others in the department. Oh, there it was. "I was exhilarated, to tell the truth. It was quite an afternoon. It's great to be in the thick of things."

"That so?" Kent's question had a barbed edge to it.

"Are you taunting me?"

"No, Caro. I'm trying to make conversation."

His enigmatic attitude had her stymied, yet a question sidled into her thoughts. If he didn't want to be here, why didn't he just leave?

Unwilling to ask that, she decided to tell him about her day at the office. "We anticipate a price move. And plan to raise prices at the pumps."

"Seems to me gasoline companies do that all the time."

"We're looking into another move. We're paying more at the refinery. We must raise prices, or lose money. We'll need one or two competitors to go along with it."

"Oil companies wouldn't want to be in the position of losing money," he said. Snidely?

She could be just as sarcastic. "Maybe we could just go to Mexico's system. Nationalize the oil companies. That should bode well for the economy and the average guy."

"It took nationalization to get ramps and parking places for the handicapped."

That went too far. Yet the crux was the same. Before laws were enacted, the plight of the physically challenged had been like Caroline's self-imposed one: isolation.

How lucky she was, leaving that wheelchair. Some folks were never so fortunate. She made a vow to herself. Somehow, someway, someday, she'd pass along the kindnesses Kent had shown.

Why tell him? Aggravating man, he'd jeered at oil companies, and mocked Caroline. She lifted her nose. "Nationalization. You sound like a socialist. Or a Boy Scout."

He laughed without mirth. "You and Lori ought to get together."

Strange, how he could turn Caroline's mind from her profession and newly pledged altruism, as well as from the previous evening's embarrassment. "Who is Lori?"

"The senior partner at Hardwicke."

A chill. A hard chill that coagulated behind Caroline's breastbone. "I suspected you had a string of babes in your pocket. Never figured you had a *boss* among them."

"Wrong. Lori's my friend, not a love interest. Never has been. We're more like brother and sister." He wiggled to face Caroline. "I've had exactly four romances. They each fit the stages of my life. College freshman, throwing off childhood. Young lawyer and a first adventure across the seas. I had a client with interests in Corsica, you see. It was natural, my falling for a French girl there.''

Her eyes ran over him. She loved his looks, the way he moved and spoke. Every gesture enticed her. If she had anything to be jealous of, it was women, American and French. They had known what he had yet to share with Caroline.

''Will I be the next number, when you kiss and tell to your next flame? Or flames.''

He cocked his head. ''Who says there'll be another?''

''Big talk, Mackay. You haven't lit my fire yet.''

Their gazes locked. It went without saying they had lit more than a flame on a certain sofa just inside the front door behind them.

Kent's eyes broke the connection first. ''Everything starts with a beginning. Just like you mentioned Frank Grant, I'm telling you. Secrets between us aren't good. I—''

''An element of mystery never hurts,'' she interrupted.

He rolled toward her, his palm cupping her leg. ''It's time to put some mysteries aside. I want you to know what goes with me. Besides those romances, I've been engaged, once. It almost got to the altar, but she balked.''

What was he saying? ''If you didn't love her, what gives?''

''She didn't ring my bell like you do.''

Bells rang in Caroline's head. ''If that's the case,

then why did you get bent out of shape? I wasn't looking to put a ring through your nose, yet you—"

"You spoke serious stuff, Caro. We need to ease back on this, make sure we won't have regrets. If you meant nothing to me, it wouldn't matter. But it does."

Last night she'd sought out his intentions. Now she knew them. They were few. Nevertheless, he cared for her and that meant something. "I don't have to marry every man I sleep with. Or am I reading my signals wrong with that, too?"

He leaned his elbows back on the porch and extended long legs. "It's inevitable. We will be together."

How smart would that be?

"It'll be good," he said. "Of that, I have no doubt."

Something tickled Caroline—her unsmart senses. Her eyes were drawn from his feet, coasting up his ankles to where his legs stopped. There was a worn place there, marking a V, marking his virility.

It was not a small spot.

"That's big of you."

"Just doing my duty as a friend, Kent." Lorraine Hardwicke's dulcet voice purred through the telephone line that connected from her downtown Dallas office to the phone in Kent's hand; he stood inside a San Antonio copy shop.

"Send the fax. I'll wait here for it."

Kent was not a happy man.

It had to do with various things. Like how he couldn't bring himself to ask, point-blank, about Caroline's admission regarding children. Like how he'd said too much last Friday night, leading her to a place she might not wish to be.

Having kept a distance from the woman he wanted, then have her in the bedroom, no cast on her leg, his hide drying on the sofa, didn't do much for his disposition. But this had to be. Only a heel would get serious with Caroline, while he was up in the air on how to handle this twist in their relationship.

It had been a long, long weekend.

Kent grabbed Natalie's hand and marched to his vehicle to wait for the fax. Once he settled the girl in her car seat, he scooted behind the wheel and banged a fist on it. Damn. He wanted Caroline. There was nothing to keep him out of her bed.

Nothing but his conscience.

What a dumb thing, telling her it was but a matter of time before they made love. He muttered a foul word. It was bad enough, being in love with her. If he once knew what it was like to join his body with hers, he feared he could never let her go.

And "go" might be exactly what she'd choose to do, if becoming a mother took precedence with her. "Dammit to hell."

"'Hell,'" Natalie mimicked clearly.

"Got to clean up my language."

But his main worries had to do with breaking the law.

Felonious acts had occupied his mind from the moment Caroline mentioned the cozy little meeting at Fill-Er-Fast. They carried forth throughout the weekend and the entirety of this morning. He'd tried to contact Hardwicke's petroleum-law expert, to no avail, then had turned to Lori. She might be a criminal-defense attorney, but her skills were well-rounded. She knew how to ferret out trouble.

Trouble was afloat.

When Kent and Natalie collected Caroline from work at five that evening, she had a bright smile and no enthusiasm for anything but Fill-Er-Fast.

She'd hopped into the Cherokee with more ability than he'd seen so far. Weekend walks through the park must have helped her.

"'O." Natalie laughed in delight.

Caroline beamed. "Guess what!"

"You got the promotion?"

"Yes!" She bounced over to lash her arms around Kent. "I'm Senior Price Analyst!"

She let go her power hug. Yet her breath, sweet with peppermint and the even sweeter hint of Caroline, tickled his senses. He'd have traded his life savings for just one kiss.

"And, oh, Kent, I can barely believe my luck."

"So...the guy got fired?"

"No. He took a job with Emerald Clover. I don't want to talk about him! Guess what! I'm going out into the world tomorrow. I have an appointment with Unitex Oil Company, at eight sharp. Just me. Filmore won't be along. Nor anyone else from the department. Just me. I'm going to signal a price movement, just as I mentioned we might."

You've got an appointment with the Exxon Valdez, *that's what you've got.*

Knowing he asked for trouble, also knowing he couldn't let her do it, Kent said, "That's against the law. Against Federal Trade Commission standards. Set your toes inside Unitex's offices and open your mouth about price fixing, and federal marshals could have your butt for antitrust violations.''

Caroline got huffy. "I beg your pardon."

"Think about it."

"Evidently you have," she said coolly.

"I smell a rat. A big, dead rat. I'll bet your predecessor got wise to Wanek—that's why he's gone to a reputable company. Wanek's banking on your inexperience. If push comes to shove, he can back off, his hands waving in innocence. He'll blame everything on you."

The shocked look in her face turned to distrust. Or was it loathing? Kent turned the key, firing the engine and pulling out of the Fill-Er-Fast parking lot.

Caroline murmured, "Filmore would never suggest anything illegal."

"Wait and see."

"Me!" came from the back seat.

Caroline unfastened her seat belt, turning to the left and around. She scrambled. Her behind tipped up as she rifled through the litter that Natalie had made on the seat beside her, Caroline provided a sight for Kent's sore eyes.

It wasn't easy, keeping his hands to himself.

Natalie started to fret.

"Where is this child's plug?" Caroline groused. "Why, at any and every crucial moment, does Natalie spout off?"

"Because she's a baby."

Having found a pacifier on the seat next to Baby, Caroline nudged it into her eager mouth.

Caroline shoved her spine against leather upholstery and refastened her seat belt. "What's with you? Wait.

Don't answer that. I know. You don't like Filmore Wanek.''

"Correct. And I don't want you cooling your heels in a federal lockup."

Shoulders sank. "You can't be right. Can't be."

Kent pulled to the side of the street to open the glove compartment. Extracting Lori's fax, he demanded, "Read it."

They arrived home, Caroline in such a state that speaking was next to impossible. She moved in a fog of disbelief, disappointment and disillusionment. Her career could be over, before it had truly begun. Unless Kent was mistaken—

"Don't be naive," he advised. "Wanek knows exactly what he's doing."

The urge to lash out, to accuse him of being high-handed died. Kent mustn't be blamed. She gathered enough presence of mind to know he'd researched antitrust laws to protect her. For that she could be thankful.

Thankful, yes, but she wasn't in a gracious mood.

She wanted to be alone, to cry without upsetting Baby. "I'm leaving," she said to Kent. "Don't expect me back tonight."

"All right."

Through the haze of confused wits, something cried out, a part cloaked in the personal rather than in business. Why didn't he try to stop her? Silly question.

Her already contracted heart squeezed and almost choked her. Kent, the come-on king, despite past innuendoes and allusions, had abdicated his throne.

She picked up the keys to her car, left the duplex and started the clunker for the drive to Canyon Lake, where she parked to stare with unseeing eyes at calm waters. It was long after dawn before she gained any sort of perspective. Over and above the situation with Kent, her chances for getting a position with another oil company were nebulous, her finances precarious, her dreams in trouble.

There was but one thing Caroline could do.

Chapter Eight

It took less than an hour to reach Fill-Er-Fast. Caroline scooted out of the car, opened her walker and advanced to Wanek's office. Cigar smoke clogged the air. Feet on his desk, elbows parked on chair arms, Filmore Wanek couldn't see his visitor, not with a glossy magazine obscuring his line of sight.

"Get me a doughnut, Mona."

"I'm not your secretary."

Sluts In Cyberspace was thrown to the floor, and his feet came off the desk. "You were supposed to be at Unitex—" he tapped cigar ashes in the vicinity of his magazine "—thirty minutes ago."

"You asked me to do something illegal."

"Who, me?" He was feigned innocence itself.

"Yes, you. And I won't do it."

His small eyes instantly flickered with anger. "Get to Unitex, or you're fired!"

"Do that." Caroline shook with indignity. "Fire me."

She turned with mustered grace and limped away. The journey to her car seemed to take a thousand minutes, as she passed co-workers and the cubicle that was her office. So much of her identity had been linked to a career in this very place. It was as if she'd experienced a death. The death of dreams.

Her head against the steering wheel, she cried. "It's over."

"I'm sorry, Caro. I wish it hadn't come to that."

"It has. Fill-Er-Fast is over for me."

Kent opened his arms and Caroline stepped into them. Dear Lord, it felt good having her here, giving her a shoulder to lean on. Taking more than he gave. Kent needed her. As flowers did rain, he needed her. And she needed him. If she could accept him, as she had accepted his scars.

"'O?"

Natalie. Tugging at her sister's skirt.

"Baby." Caroline withdrew from his embrace and lifted her sister into a hug. "Mustn't cry in front of you."

Thus she pulled herself together.

A buzzer from the kitchen drew Kent to it. He'd concocted a vegetable casserole, one he'd heard about this morning, on a TV show. It had passed a heart association's standards. He reached into the oven. Alarms went off in his senses. He'd gone for the casserole without an oven mitt.

He sucked his aching thumb.

"Cold water helps," Caroline said from behind him.

He pivoted around, letting go of his thumb. "It's not bad. Nothing. I barely touched the bowl lip. Where's Gnat Nat?"

"Watching TV." Caroline pulled on a pair of oven mitts and collected the dish, placing it atop the stove. "I think she'll stay there awhile. Would you like me to doctor this?"

A tender hand took his, turning it, turning his insides to mush.

"I'd rather you doctor—" His fingers closed over her wrist; he had it halfway to his lips before Kent caught himself. "It's a simple scorch." He lowered his arm. "No big deal."

"So you say." She went to the table, settled into a chair, idly rearranging the silverware he'd previously set. "Kent, I don't know what to do next."

"A philosopher once said, 'Acceptance is the first step in overcoming the consequences of any misfortune.'"

"That's something I do know—acceptance." Her usually bright eyes muted by too many razed ambitions, she raised a selfless question. "Has it worked for you?"

"I spent years letting scars put a chip on my shoulder. Once I got puberty behind me, I hid behind—" he pointed to his mustache "—this. Then I met you. I never see your eyes searching, as if to find out what's beneath this hair."

She blinked, her lovely mouth making an O of astonishment. "Why, Kent, I never even think about it. I see you as a whole. Not as a part."

"That's what I like the most about you." He smiled. "So the way I look at it, your acceptance got me past misfortune."

"We've helped each other, then. I can't imagine what would have happened to me, if you hadn't come along."

"Not a bad thing...friendship."

"Friendship. Yes, I guess that's what it is." She moved the sugar bowl an inch or two. "That's what we need more than anything. Someone to count on. Like Natalie counts on us."

Friendship didn't cover what Kent felt, yet he wouldn't push it, certainly not now. He made up his mind to be whatever she needed, for however long she'd want him.

"Caro, you asked what to do next. Don't do anything. Not today. Your thoughts are jumbled. Relax. Let's take an outing. We could let Natalie loose on the slides at the park."

"She's too little for letting loose. Anyhow, I didn't mean only my job. I'll find another one. Somehow," she added, unconvincingly. Anew, her gaze fastened to Kent's. "I meant, what do I do about you? Is friendship...?"

She provided an entrée to a heart-to-heart, but with Caroline vulnerable at the moment, this was the worst time to discuss the begetting of progeny. Rather, never having them.

"First things first, friend," he replied. "Don't stand on pride. I can draw a check on Natalie's account, and—"

"I want her money left intact." The old bitterness came back to Caroline's expression. "She won't be done out of it, like I was when Ruth 'borrowed' my inheritance."

"That's noble, but also foolhardy."

Eyes snapped. "How many times do I have to tell

you? I stand on my own feet." As if to prove it, she stood up without the walker's aid. "I won't touch Natalie's money."

There was no getting around this prideful woman, who added, "I must make a job of looking for one."

A week went by. The rental company picked up the walker. Caroline updated her résumé and scoured the classifieds. Every once in a while, Kent caught her staring at him, her emotions raw. He yearned to provide comfort.

This was also a week where it became apparent—pressingly so—that he must return to his Dallas office. Quickly.

At the end of that week, as the hour of ten in the evening approached, he took the newspaper from her hands and wheeled her computer chair to face him. "You're not equipped for a job search. You need to go at it with both barrels, Caro. That means a decent computer and printer. A copier. You could also use a fax and a telephone answering machine."

"Those things cost money."

Yesterday he'd pointed out that some of Ruth's estate ought to go to her, to repay a debt many years in arrears. Like now, Caroline had balked, saying if Ruth wanted to settle the debt, she would have made a proviso in her will.

Looming over her as she sat beside Mr. Ugly, Kent said, "You need to network. Or to put yourself in an executive recruiter's hands. Or to surf the Internet for opportunities."

"Mr. Ugly doesn't do the Internet. He's four years old."

"Go for personal contacts. Your chances are better in a bigger city."

"This is where I live."

"Fine. Stay here. Stay here until you're completely out of money, completely out of prospects and your sister—"

"I've saved a bit over the years. I've been frugal. I'll do fine."

"For how long?"

She glanced at the newspaper now folded next to her computer, then up at his lurking presence. "You're right. I can't do much from here."

"What's your next move?"

She clicked her tongue. Inhaled. Exhaled. Rubbed her forehead. "I can't think clearly."

"There's a home waiting for you in Plano," Kent said, knowing she'd never move into her mother's house.

"Out of the question."

"Then what is your next move?"

"What is this, Twenty Questions?"

Sometimes she could be as aggravating as her cat. "No more questions. Details. Mine. I've got to go home. Chambliss v. Snappy Sours demands my attention. And, frankly, I'm running out of allergy medicine."

"Of course you must go home," she replied, defensiveness gone. "I've hogged your time. Do go on to Dallas." Naked bravado carried her onward. "Natalie and I will be fine."

The pain in her voice began to rouse a modicum of satisfaction in Kent, selfish though it was. He wanted her to feel deeply for him, so deeply that all she'd need, outside Natalie and a decent job, was to be with him.

Knowing he trod on shaky ground, he said, "She missed her appointment with the pediatrician."

Caroline paled. "I forgot. What's the matter with me?"

"You're worried sick." He patted her shoulder, squeezing it lightly. "Don't get upset. I called Dr. McBride. She had a cancellation, two weeks from today." Which meant, if he didn't 'fess up, he had fourteen days to win Caroline's love, before it would be tested. "She'll see Natalie then."

"But Dr. McBride is in Dallas."

"Right. Dallas. Big *d,* little *a,* double *l, a-s.* That's where Gnat Nat belongs. It's where she's going to end up. She's my responsibility till you take over legally. I want her with her original pediatrician. I demand it."

"Can you do that?"

"Yes, ma'am."

"You're toying with me, Mackay." Arms folded over breasts.

"I've been about as patient as a man can be with you. But let me remind you. If you intend to keep the peace with Gnat Nat's lawyer, you *will* pack up and move to Dallas. Got it?"

Caroline's lips parted, her eyes going saucer round.

Kent took her by the elbows and raised her to stand. "You're going to move in with me."

But how long could he keep her, if she agreed? The Internet or a sharp executive recruiter might send her on a path clear out of Texas. Damn. But Kent Mackay hadn't gotten through school, then built up a successful law practice, both in record time, without being dogged and shrewd.

He would make certain her *career* kept her in Dallas.

Caroline was desperate, but not enough to kowtow to the aggravating, demanding, manipulative—arrogant—Kent Mackay. In bed, as she tossed and turned, she attributed many adjectives to him. How dare he order her around—while she was at her worst—as if she were some puppy? And the nerve of him, using Baby as a pawn. Every bit of it under the platonic flag of friendship.

By dawn, she awoke to the scent of fresh coffee. And to a realization.

Combing fingers through her hair, she meant to duck into the bathroom before facing the Commander General, but ran into him before she could do so. Naturally, he was dressed.

His eyes roamed over her oversize T-shirt, stopping on her knees. "Don't you look good," he said.

"I'll move in with you."

After she acceded to his plans, Caroline decided to concentrate on the positives, despite the friendship that was wearing thin. Moving to Dallas, into his house, would add a new dimension to their relationship. He might be demanding and arrogant, but she loved him. And she was sick of the platonic.

So, at the crack of dawn two days later, a moving van hauled her household away. Caroline, with Baby and a cat cage in tow, followed Kent Mackay's lead up I-35. Near the Dallas county line, he motioned her car to a rest area, then rolled down his window to say, "I've had a couple of phone calls. Angie won't be able to meet us at the door. She'll be along later. And,

Caro, I'll have to drop you at the house. Brush fire at the office.''

Intruding on a strange home had a daunting quality to it, but her trepidations increased once she trailed the Cherokee to Las Colinas. This was a lovely planned community of homes, offices and shops. It had grassy areas and playgrounds and ponds with fountains and ducks—much too rich for her blood.

When he drove up to the nicest high-rise and a doorman greeted him, Caroline realized something. She'd known Kent had done well for himself, but she hadn't realized how well.

Unless he was in debt up to his neck.

"Cherin will see you upstairs," Kent said, opening the car door and handing her a key to the elevator.

The doorman tipped his hat, took charge of Greezy's cage. They went past a fancy foyer and into a brass elevator that whisked upward and opened to the penthouse.

The penthouse!

"Where am I?" she said to Natalie, once Cherin left and Greezy had been let loose to roam. "What are we doing here?"

Natalie glanced at the great room, recognizing it, and looked up at her. "Kenn."

"You've got the advantage, Baby. I don't see him in this place. I picture him at home in a San Antonio duplex, not in luxury."

Holding Natalie's hand, Caroline turned a probing eye to floor-to-ceiling windows that afforded an unobstructed view of the Dallas skyline, miles to the east. It was a bird's-eye view where she could see out, but no one could see in.

French doors led to a balcony. Expensive furnishings centered the great room, a fireplace dominating the wall closest to the elevator. From a quick look around, Caroline discovered three bedrooms and more bathrooms than a bachelor would ever need. This penthouse looked like something out of a magazine, heady stuff for a working-class woman.

A buzzing sound made her jump. Following it, she found an intercom box near the elevator. "You have a visitor," Cherin announced drolly. "Ms. Lorraine Hardwicke."

"Tell her Mr. Mackay isn't here."

"She knows that. She wants to see you."

"Oh, well, okay."

What did Kent's boss want?

Lorraine "Please call me Lori" Hardwicke was just as Caroline had pictured: tall, slim and beautiful. Which, of course, made Caroline feel dumpier than an oil-storage tank. Out of place, she didn't know if it would be proper to offer the lady lawyer a refreshment or a chair. She wasn't the hostess.

But Lori eased the moment. "Do you feel as ill at ease as I do?"

Caroline nodded. "Why don't we sit down?"

Natalie between them, they sat on the boomerang-shaped sofa. No telling how many cows had been sacrificed to cover it. Greezy stalked the room, her eyes red with distrust at this strange place.

"Kit cat." Natalie climbed down to toddle after the cat.

Caroline laced fingers and tried to think of something to say, but Lori again came to the rescue. "Is this your first time living in Dallas?"

"Yes. I visited on occasion, though."

"I hope you'll come to love Big D."

"I don't know how long I'll stay. I'm looking for a job. One might take me to another city."

"Don't bank on that." Lori smoothed the skirt of her linen dress.

"I beg your pardon?"

"Kent's crazy about you. He won't let you leave the city limits, not without a fight. He's great at winning."

Sure. Right. The man for friendship had it bad. Right. If so, where was his affection? "He told you that?"

"We've worked together for eight years, been friends for most of it. I know his head. If he hasn't already, I say it won't be any time until he asks you to become a permanent part of his life."

Caroline, a hissing sound in her ears, studied the blonde. Was there a hidden meaning at work here? "Are you here to scare me off?"

"Not at all." A smile brushed Lori's perfect mouth. "I was curious. I wanted to see the woman who won Kent's heart."

"It remains to be seen what's to be won or lost, but ours isn't a game. Kent offered shelter, is all. My goal is to get a job, provide a home for Baby. And to go forth from there."

"While you're doing that, you'll need child care. A friend of mine from my Hockaday school days has a daughter. She has her enrolled at the Malagueña Preschool. It's an excellent school for early childhood development, I understand."

"I'm sure it's too expensive," Caroline replied, then recalled child-care problems would be handled by Angie Cortez.

"Too expensive? My word! Natalie Perry has enough money to attend any school, anywhere."

All along, Caroline hadn't wanted to know the scope of her sister's wealth, but within a minute or so, her eyes popped. Lori had mentioned a figure.

"That is a lot of money," Caroline uttered.

And it was net. Kent's cut of the whole was well into seven figures. Apparently he had no trouble affording anything he wanted, such as these fancy digs.

Babyish shrieks filled this hoity-toity room and veered Caroline from legal tender. They brought both women to their feet. Natalie shot from behind a game table, shaking a hand.

"Bite!"

Hackles raised, Greezy ran straight at a windowpane. She went airborne. A thump thudded through the room as she hit glass. Tumbling backward, the tortie did a midair gyration that landed her on paws.

"Heeeeehhhhh," Greezy announced and shook herself.

"She hates being off the ground floor." Caroline wrung her hands. "She's used to trees outside the windows and having birds to taunt. There're eight floors between us and the nearest tree or bird."

"We'll figure something out." Lori had ideas. An aquarium with a top, filled with colorful fish. A cage of gerbils. "I don't recommend gerbils, though. I tried them with my own cats, but I ended up with a colony of rodents."

Somehow Caroline couldn't picture this cool lady with cats or gerbils, or cleaning up after them.

"What did you do?" she asked.

Natalie, tired of being ignored and still smarting

over the cat bite, tugged on Caroline's hand. "Me!
'O?"

"She's a precious child," Lori commented as Caroline picked her up.

"I think so." Caroline then asked, "What do you
say to seeing if Kent has some coffee?"

"Sounds good to me."

They went to the kitchen and got coffee brewing.
Natalie settled in a chair, enjoying a sipper-cup of
juice. Caroline asked, "What did you do about the
gerbils?"

Lori stirred no-fat creamer into her cup. "It was
Halloween. What else could I do but give trick-or-
treaters a choice between candy or a gerbil?"

"You didn't!" Caroline laughed, acknowledging a
hoyden behind the poised bearing. "I love it!"

"Only got one back."

"And what did you do with the returnee?"

A hum in her throat, Lori had mischief in her features. "I did what any self-respecting defense attorney
would do. I let it loose in the D.A.'s office."

"You wicked, wicked thing!" Caroline said with a
laugh.

"Well, what would you have done?"

"With half your craftiness, exactly the same."

It had been building up for several minutes, but Caroline knew right then: she liked Lori Hardwicke. They
would be friends, good friends.

Lori was a great introduction to Dallas.

Even though Greezy remained an unhappy camper,
Caroline had another pleasant introduction to the north
Texas city. Angie Cortez was as winsome as Kent had
promised. The pretty, petite lady, her long dark hair

swirled in a knot at the crown of her head, looked forward to her new responsibilities, and it showed, from the way she cuddled "Natacita," to her enthusiasm for taking Baby on a tour of the grounds.

Not long after they left, Kent returned, a bouquet of red roses in hand. "These are for you. Put 'em beside your bed, okay?"

Caroline didn't quite know what to think, but she decided to take the roses as a good sign.

Then the van arrived with her worn-out furnishings. She locked the cat in the utility room to keep her quiet during the move-in. If not quiet, at least confined.

In concert with the furnishings that said "decorator" in tall letters, Kent balked at allowing Caroline's furnishings into his home—they got assigned to public storage on Highway 183. Except for one item. "Set up that iron bed in the bedroom, left side of the hallway," he ordered the movers.

As she arranged the roses in a vase on the bedside table, once the movers were gone, she wanted to ask if they were meant in friendship or more, but Kent posed a question.

"Caro, did you and Frank sleep together in this bed?"

This was the first time in days he'd spoken on a familiar level. That, with roses... Rather than jump in with both feet, like she'd done that night in the duplex, she walked to a window to stare at the buttermilk sky. "My dad had this bed as a boy. I used it as a girl. Frank preferred a water bed. But yours wasn't a fair question, not even between friends."

"True." A moment passed before he changed the subject. "Looks like everything is set. In record time, too."

She turned to see Kent dust his hands, having shoved the bed to face the window. Movers didn't think about that sort of thing.

Clearly uncomfortable, he glanced at the watch strapping his wrist. "Three-thirty. I've got time enough for a shower before I go back to the office. Will you be okay here alone?"

"Of course." With Natalie on that tour, emptiness went through Caroline. She missed her little angel. But she and Kent both agreed Baby must be weaned from their round-the-clock presence. They would return at five. "I'll just putter around."

"Didn't I tell you Angie would be pleased to trade her apron to become a nanny?" he asked confidently, having previously called a cleaning service to do the dirty work.

"She does seem awfully nice."

He proceeded to pick up the photo of Caroline's father that she'd arranged on the dresser. "Seems strange having a family picture sitting around."

For all his success he'd never known a father's love—even the rich could be poor. Caroline felt for that void in his background. Here lately she hadn't given much support.

"I wish it could have been different for you," she whispered and hugged the arms exposed beneath her sleeveless top.

"I know you do, Caro. Like understands like." He set the photo down to smile. "I'd better get that shower."

"I'd better see if I can connect to the Internet."

Her voice lacked enthusiasm, as did her spirit. Whenever she'd read the classifieds, she'd seen behind the small print to some weasel asking her to do the unethical or illegal. The idea of oil companies had never lured her, truth be known. She'd thought experience in a refinery would benefit her in the industry. Humph. It left a taste as sour as six-oil.

Nevertheless, she had to do something. Already she'd made an appointment for next week with a headhunter. Why not get ready for it? "Kent, what did you do with my box of résumés?"

"Look in the office. It's next to the computer."

She nodded and passed him, making for the home office situated on the other side of the apartment. What a place. Such bounty. It was almost enough to make her smile.

The office had ambience. It bespoke attention to Kent's profession, with a smathering of personal items—a certificate here, an award there. Apparently he knew how to hoist a bowling ball. He had the ticky-tacky treasures to show for it; they made her smile. Like the gerbil story had humanized Lori, so did the bowling trophies close the gap between Caroline and a hotshot lawyer.

She carried on nosing around. The latest in computers nestled amid a walnut suite of furniture, the likes of which she'd never before seen with her own two eyes. She also saw machines for copying, faxing and printing. Tall stacks of law reviews, along with history books and general fiction, lined the shelves. A closet held office supplies, a wet bar the finest in liquors; a discrete ice machine was tucked away near a refrigerator filled with an assortment of soft drinks and bottled water. Next to a leather easy chair, and its requisite long sofa, was a stack of magazines that appealed to lawyers and businessmen. Not a single copy of *Sluts in Cyberspace* was among the stack.

There was a book on baby care beside them, though.
But where was her stuff?

She traversed to the bedroom wing. "Kent?" The
door to his bedroom was closed. "Kent?"

"It's not locked. Come in."

She did. Her mouth went dry.

He stood in front of a chest of drawers. Black hair
damp and ruffled, he twisted toward her and glanced
over a shoulder. He wore nothing but a towel that
wrapped lean hips, white terry cloth contrasting with
the rich bronze of his skin.

In the weeks they lived in her cramped duplex, he'd
been careful about dressing behind a closed bathroom
door "for Gnat Nat's sake." Natalie wasn't home...at
the moment.

He closed the drawer and tossed a pair of cotton
briefs to the bed, the muscles in his upper body rip-
pling with lean grace...reminding her of the true reason she'd agreed to this move. To be with Kent.

To try to recapture the magic he'd elicited, before
he took it away. If he were interested, like Lori alluded
to, why didn't he smile? Why wasn't he crossing the
room to kiss her? What sort of reassurance did he
need?

Or was this punishment for her drink-loosened lips?

"Something wrong?" he asked and took a brush to
his hair.

"I—I, no." *Get your eyes off his chest. Off the tufts
growing beneath his arms.* "I—I need to find my
things."

She pivoted, and flew out of there as fast as her
lousy legs could carry her, almost stumbling over the
box that sat by the office door. Why hadn't she seen

it before? It was probably some sort of psycho thing. Like, not wanting to see it.

Slumped in the big chair in front of his computer, she fell to a pity party. She'd never imagined herself being so messed up in the head about a man, much less one as attractive as Kent Mackay.

What had gone wrong between them?

Before she could form an answer, she caught sight of him from the corner of her eye. He was dressed now. Magnificently so. Garbed in the sort of suit that cost more than she spent on clothes in a year, he wore a starched white shirt and a tie that had to be the best of silks.

He also wore a frown. "If this situation is going to succeed, I think you and I should talk."

"I think so, too."

Closing the door and striding to the desk, he leaned a hip down on it. They were close enough that the sandalwood cologne got to her.

She swept her wits into a tidy pile in her brain. "Kent, you've changed." She hoped he'd step in any second to correct her, as she said, "Ever since that night I had too much to drink and got maudlin, you've been different. I thought we had something going, just me and you. Beyond friendship."

"You scare me, Caro."

A big, fat leaden ball plunked into her stomach. "You're simply not interested."

He shifted closer and tilted her chin, his blue eyes shadowed by...sadness? remorse? "You're wrong if you think I don't want you."

"What's stopping you?"

The finger that had tilted her chin now dropped to his side. "I think your heart was talking that night, not liquor. You want what most women want. You want it all. Nothing wrong with that. It's a great concept. But I wonder what you'll settle for.''

She couldn't help the rueful laugh that tickled her chest. "I'm sitting here, a beggar in a man's home. Unemployed. Pushing thirty-two, no job experience to brag about. A little girl depending on me for the next no-telling-how-many years. I'd settle for a job." *And for you.* But that wouldn't be settling. Having Kent would be like grabbing the proverbial brass ring. "Will you let me take back those things I said that night…?"

"How serious were you about your dreams?" He shifted to stand above her. "Answer me, Caro."

Desire played havoc with her crumbling sanity, yet a scrap of sense surfaced. "I realize most of my dreams will never come true. It could be worse. I could be in a Monte Vista duplex, expecting my happiness to come from Fill-Er-Fast."

"Those days are over."

"And I'm left with Baby. Can't say I've gotten shorted. She's fabulous. I am blessed."

"That's good to hear. But what did you mean about having children?"

His question startled her. Lately she'd assumed his hesitation had to do with nose rings, not kids. It was all she could do not to laugh. Here they were, sexual vibes zapping between them, and they discussed procreation? "I would assume, since you graduated from several affairs without becoming a father, you know at least the rudiments of pregnancy prevention."

"I do."

So why didn't he *act?* How could he simply lean there against that stupid desk?

"Damn you, Kent Mackay! Kiss me."

Chapter Nine

Caroline, proud Caroline, wanted a kiss, and more. So did Kent. While she hadn't eased his mind on no-kids-forever, he had to accept reality. It would be foolish in the least, and unkind at the most, giving in to urges. Unfortunately, Kent couldn't think with his head.

And the control he'd kept intact this long, slipped.

Filing everything but the moment into the deepest recesses of his mind, he had her out of the chair in no time. His lips took hers. Their tongues met, anything but mildly. The bends of his knees touched the desk, and he relished the feel of her soft curves at his front. Then she was between his spread legs, knowing what passion did to him.

They were meant to make love.

At first his fingers slipped into her hair and gently disturbed her ponytail. He twined the loosened strands, loving them. "Beautiful hair. I've missed touching it. I've yearned for more of what we had on that couch in your living room."

"We have wasted time."

"But no more." He carried her to the sofa, placed her on it, knowing he must leave for a moment to prepare himself, but he couldn't stand the thought of that moment being this one.

"Mmm," she purred, the backs of her naked arms and calves to the sofa. "Oh, Kent, how well we fit together."

Again they kissed. This one went beyond tangled tongues. He coasted his lips along her cheek, across her eyelid, over to her ear. Her pelvis pressed his. That was when her fingers fiddled beneath his jacket, urging him out of it.

"You're warm," she murmured.

"Yeah. And you haven't even gotten to the source."

"Shall I?"

"No. I'm first."

"Doctor wants to examine the patient?" she teased, recalling his long-past request, while he tugged her clothes away and ran hungry hands along her satiny skin.

"Something like that."

What he wanted was to reacquaint his senses with her flesh and to explore the secrets as yet unmined. Most of all, he wanted her satisfaction. It meant more than his own.

But... "I'm selfish," he uttered, reveling in her shapely legs, her plump-to-perfection hips, the nip of her waist, even her navel. "It intrigues me, your in-nie."

His fingers caressed her breasts. "Beautiful breasts." Rounded with cinnamon centers, they swelled in his hands and beckoned his lips. "You taste better than cinnamon." Kent did like cinnamon.

Her pelvis bucked, after he suckled one crest and had moved to the other. "Touch me everywhere," she entreated.

He answered by combing four fingers through the web of hair at her mound. He slipped into her moist folds, groaning at the feel. She sizzled. His finger moved in the rhythm of lovemaking, and almost instantaneously, the sizzle became a conflagration.

Wanting to see her reaction, he gazed at her face. Teeth bared, eyes glazed, she rode his hand. And he had to take a deep breath, or else he'd embarrass himself.

"'O! Kenn!"

"Yoo-hoo, anybody here?"

Caroline and Kent sprang apart. Trying to catch his breath, he said, "Looks like Gnat and Angie are home early."

And it was for the best. Not only because he hadn't had the cleverness of schoolboys who kept foil packets in their wallets. Because it was wrong to make love to Caroline, when he had secrets to confess.

She fiddled with her hair. "I'm going to loan Angie my watch. So she'll know two hours from three."

"Things happen for a reason." He boosted her fingers to his cheek, the mustache brushing the edge of her hand. "I need to know you totally accept me, before I get too attached to you."

"How many times do I have to reassure you?"

"Shhh. Look, honey, when I return from the office, there's something we need to discuss."

"I'm tired of talking."

He slipped an arm around her shoulders, his closed fist nudging her jaw toward his face. "When we do this thing, and I'm not talking about talking, I want it to be in that iron bed of yours. I'm a man of fantasies. I want to hear those springs, each time we move."

"Maybe all our fantasies will come true."

They quickly got into their clothes.

There was no time for fantasies, yet Caroline kept grinning over what had happened, even though it had been cut short. She had never been one for an easy climax. Then, she had never before had the pleasure of Kent. She expected even greater satisfaction, later tonight.

For now he left for his office; she greeted Baby and her nanny. Angie Cortez, despite an inability to track time, was a plum.

"'O!" Smiling and showing adorable teeth, as well as dancing blue eyes, Natalie flailed her arms.

Angie gave Natalie over to her sister's arms, asking, "We had a good time, didn't we, Natacita?"

"'Gie." Natalie turned a rosy-cheek smile on her nanny.

Caroline nuzzled Baby's neck and savored the smell of sunshine and a tiny, sweet child. Only one other person felt this good to hold. And they were different, of course. Natalie, precious Natalie, was soft and little, innocent and pure.

"I've missed you." That wasn't altogether true, Kent having kept her occupied, but having Angel Baby back pointed out how lonely a few minutes could be.

* * *

That evening, after Angie went home, Caroline prepared a dilled-salmon dinner, then slipped into her best dress-up outfit. She found candles. She located wine and wineglasses, and selected a Côte du Rhone, even though she hadn't the slightest idea if it was as good as Texas wine, which she liked. She slipped vintage Billie Holiday, and the more contemporary Luther Vandross and Quincy Jones, into Kent's CD player. Okay, she had a few problems figuring out how to get the music going, but she did it, eventually. The mood was set.

Too bad Greezy, out for revenge, clawed her stockings.

Too bad Baby refused an early supper and bed.

Too bad Kent showed up, at nine, with shopping bags that held a collection of pet gear. "Bought Greezy an aquarium and fish." Like a kid, he lofted plastic bags of colorful aquatics. "Bought her a kitty condo, too. All we have to do is set it all up, then she'll be happy. I hope."

Caroline bit down on a glower. After what had happened this afternoon he had Greezy on his mind? Could be worse. "There's some assembly required," she said.

He smiled sheepishly. "I was hoping you'd lend a hand."

She eyed the chore. "Where do you keep your toolbox?"

"Toolbox?"

"You know, screwdrivers and such."

He paled. "I don't own a screwdriver."

"I should've figured as much." Caroline lunged for Natalie, who clamped fingers around a plastic bag of guppies and was shaking them. "No, no, Angel Baby."

Natalie went for the fish her sister rescued. "Mine!"

Kent reached into his pocket and pulled out a chocolate bar. "Here, Gnat Nat. Enjoy."

"She hasn't had dinner."

"Have you got a better suggestion?"

"Unwrap that candy."

Natalie set forth to enjoy her treat, rubbing it in the usual places. Kent tore into boxes, got the aquarium atop a shelf in the utility room and Caroline went to the kitchen for a butter knife. The aquarium project proceeded without disaster, but assembling the kitty condo didn't prove as fortunate.

Twice, Caroline banged her fingers, her mind being preoccupied with a hunk who sat and watched her work. She kicked off her shoes. Hiked up her skirt. Took better charge of the butter knife and put the thing to rights.

Greezy turned up her nose at the new home, ignored the fish and roosted atop an air cleaner.

Baby fell asleep, covered in chocolate, on the floor. What a satisfying evening...

"I'll put her to bed," Kent offered.

"She needs a bath and something decent to eat."

"Caro, leave it go for once. It's been a long day."

"No joke. Put her to bed."

He scooped Natalie up and went toward her bedroom. Caroline made a beeline for the dining room to down a whole glass of Côte du Rhone, which had a calming effect. Another glass had her rolling shoulders in time to Billie Holiday. The French did have a way with wine!

"You hungry?" Kent asked from the archway.

Limpid eyes settled on a dreamboat who'd gotten rid of his tie and had loosened a pair of shirt buttons. "For you."

"Are you drunk?"

"Might be."

"Drink does loosen your tongue." A frown became a smile. "Maybe that won't be all bad."

"Want some wine?" she asked and moistened her lips.

"I'll have cognac."

"Me, too."

"Let's sit in the great room," he suggested.

At the wet bar he poured two snifters from a decanter and placed them on the octagonal table cupped by the sofa. Caroline settled into the leather, and tucked bare feet beneath her. Kent sat well away from her.

She noted tiredness in his eyes. The fingers of one hand going to his mustache, he shelved his upper lip. "What's wrong, Kent? Too much 'assembly required'?"

"No. It's the hazards of being a lawyer."

This wasn't going well. It sobered her. "Want to talk about it?"

"Who do I have to talk to, if not you?" His eyes softened, mellowed by the lights of Dallas beyond. "I got rich, representing people like your mother. Sometimes I hate my work."

"And...?"

"We had a meeting, the folks from Snappy Sours and the fellow who's suing them. My client will win, if it gets to court. Lew Chambliss doesn't have a good lawyer. I'm sickened."

"You're in business to win."

"I don't like rolling over a quadriplegic." Kent set his brandy snifter on the low table, got up from the sofa, then repositioned himself on it. Next to Caroline.

Greezy settled on the spot he'd abandoned and glared at him. Kent stroked Caroline's hand. "Seeing you in a wheelchair gave me a conscience."

He shifted toward her, his arm going around her waist. Sandalwood had evaporated; the enticing, pure scent of Kent remained. Relishing it, she placed a hand on his leg. His warmth heated her palm. A sexy voice emitted from the stereo speakers, singing about body heat.

"Right now, Caro, I need you as a sounding board."

Don't get frustrated, she told herself, but she couldn't help it.

"I've got to do something to offset the way I make a living."

"Why don't you represent people like Mr. Chambliss?"

"I don't want to end up a storefront lawyer."

Recalling her weeks-old vow to return his kindness by doing for another helpless person, she suggested, "Donate energy and money to causes for the handicapped."

"Not a bad idea. But I don't have time to spare. The extra I steal, I intend to spend with you and Gnat Nat."

"Donate money, and give me your time." Deciding it was now or never, she stretched to her feet. Hips swaying, she headed for her bedroom, throwing over a shoulder, "Starting now."

Caroline didn't need to throw far. Kent was right

behind her, pulling her against his front, fingers slipping into her hair. The soft stream of his breath tickled her ear, rousing a frisson of anticipation. He murmured, "You'd try the patience of a monk. And as you can tell—" hips thrust upward, speaking an ancient language known since time began "—I've lost control where you're concerned."

Chapter Ten

Before now, Caroline considered satin sheets extravagant. Not now. Not after Kent stripped off her dress, kissing each exposed part, and had dragged his shirt from wide shoulders. No, not an extravagance, she decided, the beat of evocative music in the background, lush fabric at her back...his chest hair tickling her front.

"Let's get free of this," he murmured and rid her of the lacy bra she'd saved for special occasions.

Fingers strong yet gentle covered her breasts, caressing them with care; her pulse swirled in the most delicious way from his touch. He reared his head, the lights of Dallas a backdrop, the darkened bedroom making a silhouette of his form. It was as if she suddenly owned the whole of Dallas.

She'd tell him so, once she was saner. Right now... "Shouldn't I take off my panties?"

"That's my job." Fingertips sank beneath elastic and tugged the underwear from her hips. The best pair of French-cuts she owned flew toward the lights of Big D.

"God, you're beautiful," he whispered in a ragged tone. "Like a goddess."

She knew she wasn't special. That he thought her thus brought a thrill. "Never have I seen a more beautiful man."

Yet he flipped away. Would he do his exit bit again? He reached for one of the thornless roses on the table beside this bed, and heady anticipation replaced panic. He tickled her nose with the velvety flower.

She giggled. And wiggled.

"You're great at wiggling," he murmured and drew a petally line along her collar bone. "I love the way you wiggle your butt when you walk."

"I like the way you walk, too," she said. "You're like one fluid line. So sensual."

"Coming from a tigress, I'll take that as a compliment."

However he took her compliment, he renewed his erotic assault. The tip of the rose tickled her ear, her nose, the area between her breasts. Then he made a circle around the crest of one; it tightened, aching with need.

"Quit teasing," she moaned, her insides afire when he tugged the petals from their bud and cupped them in his palm.

"But I've just begun, sweetheart."

He kneaded flowers into her warm, willing flesh, teasing without mercy, giving attention to each pleasure point. Never again would she see a rose and not think about this moment.

Oh, how lovely it was. Wondrous, dreamy. It was a haze she indulged in. Would she recall each nuance, each kiss, each whisper? She prayed so. Yet when his lips touched her femininity she lost rational thought. His skilled tongue brought her to a thundering spasm that left her panting for the act of completion.

His long lean body coasted upward, giving her a look at his divine face before he moved his lips to her ear. Whispering into it, he gave kisses between syllables. "I've wanted to be in this bed with you. Yearned to touch you and taste and feel you. And hear you moan my name when I take you."

"Oh, Kent, why did we wait?"

He stilled. "Caro, you must understand—"

"Don't do this. Don't absent yourself. You've done that too much." Her fingers gripped his shoulders. "What is it going to take to…to make these springs creak?"

"Tart—wonderful, lusty tart," he growled, and she felt his smile against her cheek. "But, Caro, you may have regrets."

"Don't tell me what I want, or what I should think. I've been obsessed with you since that day you showed up at the duplex, carrying Baby and making demands. I'm making my own demands. Dammit, Kent, take off your trousers."

He chuckled, working his zipper. In one shifting motion he shoved suit pants and briefs down his long, long legs.

It didn't escape her notice that he took something from a pocket before the trousers fell, and shoved it beneath a pillow. And then he kissed her again, rolling her under him. They became even more frenzied in their passion for each other. The old bed creaked.

"Now, Kent. Now!"

As she clutched at him, he captured her hands in one of his, anchoring them above her head. "Patience, my sweet."

Breathless, writhing, she knew, in some part of her boiling brain, that he took measures to control the possible consequences of what they were about to do. Then the bed moaned loudly.

Or was it her own moan?

He was in her, completely, fully...and the sounds of ancient springs sang in melody with the frantic needs of her body. At last they were one. Completely, totally one. Her legs wrapped around him, his palms sliding beneath her shoulder blades, his lips gliding to her throat, the sensitive place behind her ear, then finding her mouth eager for their kiss. And all the while, the springs groaned.

He plunged deeper and deeper, again and again. "I—I'm flying," she said, probably shouting.

"Hold tight, sweetheart. This ride has just begun."

Fearing she'd sail from his loving, she grasped the iron rails above her head. The breasts she presented were lavished, even though the tempo didn't ebb.

Once more she reached the stars, and they exploded behind her eyes. He slowed for a moment. Only a moment. "My lover, my love," she moaned.

Although celibate for quite a while, he showed magnificent control. Control that always seemed on the edge of slipping as he brought her to heavens never before discovered. But he didn't slip. This bliss did not end too soon.

He had never, ever been this satisfied, had never known this much calm and peace. Nor had he ever been this eager for another trip on the roller coaster with Caroline.

She remained in his arms, still joined to him, as they cuddled, her leg thrown over his thighs. He kissed her temple, then the wingtip of an eyebrow. He wanted her again. But somewhere in the back of his mind, the voice of his conscience raged at him. *Before you got past control, you should've told her everything.*

It seemed an insult to make love to her, then run his mouth. How could he confess he'd betrayed her trust, while still in her bed, her lush body having answered his fantasies?

He turned to his back, resting against a soft pillow. For a long moment he stared at the skyline shining through the tall window; then he turned his face toward Caroline's soft, satisfied countenance. "You make me a happy man."

She smiled. "Sir, like you, I live to serve."

They shared a chuckle.

He bent to take care of the contraceptive. For a moment his hand froze. He jackknifed to a seated position, praying what he feared wasn't true. It was.

"Dammit to hell," he muttered through clenched teeth.

Caroline canted toward him, her fingers curving around his waist. "What's wrong?"

"The damn thing broke."

"I—I thought so."

"Why didn't you say something?" He squeezed his eyes closed, slumping, barely feeling the warmth of her leg. "Caro, what if you're pregnant?"

"What if I am?"

"A child is the last thing I want."

"Don't overreact," she said patiently. "It wouldn't be the end of the world."

"It would be to me."

He felt the chill that went through her body, cooling the room as if a blue norther arrived. Bending over, she tossed trousers atop his knees. Crushed petals drifted to the floor.

"I believe these are yours," she said, her voice way too even. "Put them on. And get out of here."

He tried to stand, yet his fingers curled around the mattress edge. "Let me know if there's a repercussion."

"I ought to kick your butt straight off this bed."

He shoved one foot into a trouser leg, then the other. Standing, he yanked his zipper. "Don't bother. I'm leaving."

Thus he made his way slowly across the hall, to his own bedroom. *You should've told her why you won't chance a child.* How foolish he'd been at the onset, thinking his deep secrets would never create problems.

Caroline may have accepted his thin-skinnedness about the scars of his youth, but he couldn't bring himself to tell her the truth. About the research he'd done into the man and woman who'd caused his birth, and their present circumstance.

Moreover, like his father, Kent had been born with the cleft-palate deformity. Theirs was a lousy-genes cocktail.

Having Caroline recoil would be a thousand times worse than anything that had happened in his past.

He devastated her. After Kent tore off to his room, leaving her with the memory of his rotten behavior, Caroline didn't know what hurt the most. His rejection. Or his repulsion at the thought of having a child with her.

Why had he gotten so bent out of shape? Up to now, he'd always been attentive, interested in anything pertaining to her, as well as to Baby. What had made him change? What had made the idea of an accident so repugnant?

"I don't know," she whispered to the darkened ceiling of her borrowed bedroom. "I just don't know."

Maybe he was scared of a shotgun wedding. She wasn't keen on it, either, but wouldn't take it out on the child.

How did one deal with a man like Kent? Love affairs were as foreign to her as the Swahili language, yet she wasn't ignorant enough to think that she was the first woman to be disappointed in matters of the heart.

Cold comfort.

Needing to rid herself of his scent, she drew a hot bath and sank into a pity party. If she hadn't let Ruth bilk her out of Daddy's insurance money... If she hadn't been a ninny, running to Frank and marrying him for security... If she'd been a smart cookie and gone to college right after high school... If she'd simply listened to the brains she had, first off, she wouldn't have been vulnerable to Kent. Nor made a fool of herself, begging for sex.

If, if, if.

She got out of the tub, reached for a towel and wrapped it around her. Tired of being gullible, she would get to the bottom of at least one thing.

Kent's bedroom wasn't far from hers. She didn't bother to knock. Shoving the door open, she saw him, dressed in his suit pants, staring out at the night view of airborne planes from DFW airport.

"If there is a repercussion," she said without preamble, "you'd better not dare suggest I do anything about it."

He pivoted toward her, his expression in the shadows. "That's noble. And selfish. You've got your career to consider. And your hands full with Natalie."

A thousand names to call him, none decent, came to mind, but she settled on the biggest insult of all. "Why, Kent Mackay, if I didn't know better, I'd think you were Ruth Perry's son!"

She stomped back to her room, turning the lock. After burying her head in a pillow that smelled too much like Kent, she wondered if she hadn't overreacted. Any sane man, any nineties guy with a scrap of PS, looked out for untimely pregnancies. She ought to be glad.

No way.

Frank had humiliated her by being repulsed with the idea of fathering her children. Okay, she was touchy.

What a relief, finding Kent gone the next morning, before she got the gumption to leave her room. She could take only so many confrontations. It was good, Natalie's need for care; she kept Caroline too occupied to think about last night.

"Gotta have coffee," she told the toddler dressed in bows and a pink romper.

The minute she brought the first restorative sip to her lips, what had been the gates of hell turned to an inferno.

It started with an innocent-enough buzz from Cherin, who put on a Yankee-sounding man. "Delivery for Mr. Mackay.'' She'd ride down to accept it. Since Angie wasn't expected for another hour, she scooped Natalie up and entered the elevator. As soon as brass doors slid open on the ground floor, a camera flashed.

The blind spots in Caroline's eyes hadn't dissolved before a man shoved a business card into her hand. "Nice to meet you, Ms. Grant. I'm Art Garrison, *Enquiring Eye*."

The tabloids had sniffed out Natalie's story.

By the time she got free from the reporter, and Angie had arrived, Caroline knew she had to face Kent.

It would have been more palatable, downing a straight shot of leaded gasoline, rather than calling on his ritzy office. The previous night was too fresh in Caroline's memory, but Natalie's welfare carried her on.

A grand place was the downtown Hardwicke Law Firm. Wood paneling, crisp lines, leather furniture, just the right touches of greenery. A receptionist whisked Caroline past secretaries to a corner office that had a view to rival Kent's penthouse.

His back was to her as Caroline walked in. An Italian suit stretched snugly at his shoulders, his arms being crossed tightly in front of him.

The receptionist, quietly and professionally, stepped aside and closed the door, leaving Caroline and Kent alone.

When she spoke his name, he turned. For a moment caught in time, each forgot the problems that separated them. She sensed his thoughts were like hers, about last night. Before it turned sour. When they had made love with rose petals between them, antique springs squeaking, their bodies fused as one.

A child is the last thing I want.

His words, rearing up in her memory like a mad beast, broke the spell. Into the silence, she said, "We have a problem."

Before he got the wrong idea, she went on. "The tabloids know about Baby. The *Enquiring Eye* intends to run a story." How loathsome, that she'd once read such trash with glee. "Something like 'Miracle Baby Now An Orphan—and An Heiress.'"

"I know."

"Then why are you standing there? Why aren't you doing something about it!"

"Keep your voice low. Sit down. Thank you. The reporter came here. I've been trying to get in touch with you. Where have you been?"

"That's not important right now. I'd like to know how that awful man found out about Baby in the first place. Who told him? Do you have any idea?"

"We had a temp working here while I was gone. She came across the file. Her agency is firing her, as we speak."

"Cold comfort." How many more such comforts were on the horizon? "What can we do to protect Baby? I won't have her growing up an oddity. The butt of conception jokes. Sign a check, Kent. A big check." Where she'd once had too much pride to touch the child's money, Caroline was desperate. "I'm going to take her away. Far from here."

Kent strode forward, fingers clamping the armrests, his bared teeth in her face. "No."

"Yes."

"You're not taking her away. No judge has given

you legal custody. For now, I'm acting on her behalf. Caro, she needs you and me.''

"There's no more 'you and me.'''

He straightened, stepped back. Blue eyes went hard. "Just so there's no misunderstanding, let me hear it from your lips. You don't want me because I had a fit over what happened?"

He looked at her as if she had oozing sores and six noses. She wanted to hate him, but couldn't. Nor could she lend any sort of support. "Let's get something straight, Mackay. I don't have a father to push you to the altar by way of a shotgun barrel. But I'm pretty doggone good at looking out for myself. If last night turns out as badly as you fear, I'll be good at looking out for our child.''

"You don't know what you're saying," he uttered, the tan of his face having grayed.

Disappointed that he hadn't tried to reassure her, she charged, "You're no better than your father, repulsed at the idea of his own child.''

"Then we are at an impasse," he said, but she knew she'd cut him to the quick, comparing Kent to the cur who'd left a flawed baby to the welfare system.

But she had to think of Natalie. And herself. "Whip out Baby's checkbook. I need money, lots of it. I demand it now.''

"You're not taking her away."

"I am.''

He retreated to the edge of his desk. Tugging the knee of a trouser leg, he sat and turned a castigating eye, saying, "How like Ruth, to run at the first sign of trouble.''

"That is a low blow.''

"I didn't get rich, underestimating my opponents.''

She yearned to smack him upside the head, perhaps with a two-by-four. *Calm down.* After all, he'd spoken the truth on both scores. And if she ran, she'd be acting like her mother.

He went on. "You have no legal rights. I'm exercising mine. Natalie stays. And if you want to be part of her life, you stay, too. At the penthouse."

"Blackmailer."

"'Blood tells,' to use one of your expressions."

A shiver ran the length of her spine, bile rising in her throat. "You sicken me."

That was when he abandoned his deceptively casual pose to cross the office and jerk her to him. Her head tilted back; she glared at his rigid countenance. What had been subzero eyes now showed pure suffering.

"I should sicken you. I'm a rat and a louse, and I don't have it in me to change. But I'm crazy about you, Caro. You're my first true love. And hopefully my last. I don't have much to offer, but I don't want to lose you. I refuse to let you go."

When did his hands slide up her arms? When did his fingers dislodge her ponytail? When did it all turn to passion? Those things happened, before his mouth took hers.

She wilted, yet he'd hurt her deeply. She pulled away. "If you didn't want me shouting, you surely don't want this to progress, and have the secretaries giggling outside your door. Besides, I doubt you've bought heavy-duty—"

"Enough."

"I won't shut up. Not until we've settled a few things." She traveled over the carpet. "If you won't allow Baby to leave—and, believe me, I'm not going if she can't—then you need to tell me exactly what you have in mind.''

"We stay status quo until after probate court. Then—''

"What about the *Enquiring Eye?*''

"You leave Art Garrison to me.''

Strangely, Caroline trusted Kent to take care of the media insect. Not that she'd admit it.

"Then," he continued, "I find a different place. One with a yard, and all that jazz.''

"During the jazz, I'm supposed to shack up with you?''

"If you want more of what we had in the earlier part of last night, yes. If you're willing to take birth-control pills.''

"You forget a step in this cozy package. What if it's too late for pills?''

"Let's don't borrow trouble.''

Her teeth clamped together so hard that they hurt. "You've won this battle," she managed to utter. "But it's not over, if it's too late for pills.''

Caroline knew how to make Kent feel like forty kinds of a heel. He had it coming, of course. He deserved her wrath. With the Art Garrison complication, along with Snappy Sours, he couldn't devote his energies to making things right with the woman he loved, but by the next Tuesday morning, he had decided to give Caroline the benefit of the doubt.

He found her in the breakfast room, poring over the newspaper. It went without saying she looked for mentions of her sister. So far, Kent hadn't been able to stop the *Enquiring Eye* machine.

"'Morning," he said gruffly.

She folded the paper. Her gaze, hollowed by hurt, met his. A terrible pain lanced him for bringing that hurt.

"You could have spared me your hissy fit," she said quietly. "I started my period this morning."

Blowing the air from his lungs, he drooped in relief to a chair. His relief was short-lived. They had gotten a break, but what would happen next month? Kent had lived thirty years without the hot pleasures of Caroline. Still and all, another thirty days, even thirty minutes, seemed too much to consider. To look at her without remembering their shared pleasure, without wanting more of it, was beyond him. He just couldn't think above his belt.

He had to use his head. If they were to reach beyond their rift, that meant candor. "Caro, I—"

"Lots in the paper today," she said nervously. "Fill-Er-Fast got caught with their pants down."

Kent didn't give a damn about Fill-Er-Fast, but he had to polish some rough edges. "How do you feel about that?"

"Sad." She took a sip of orange juice. "The world is full of trouble, isn't it? This person's misfortune, that person's bad judgment. I was reading a story..."

How could she sit here, yammering about newspaper articles, when their relationship was so tenuous? *Don't be stupid.* Nervousness made her chatter. Kent would be patient.

"...awful people," she was saying. "How safe is Natalie from herself? Kent, her biological mother the same as sold her. Her father's parents—no telling what they're like. It gives me the creeps, thinking about Baby turning out badly. We're all products of our parents."

She wasn't making a lot of sense with her rantings about Natalie's future. Could be Kent wasn't hearing right. His mind was clear on one thing: Caroline did believe that blood told.

Unable to look her in the eye, Kent got the hell out of the breakfast room. He had his reasons. Fate's hand had turned the cards, showing aces and eights. Dead man's hand. They were doomed as a couple.

"You need to hide."

"You're right, we need to hide," Caroline answered Lori, even though Kent had sued for reason: that she not go ballistic over the latest twist in their situation.

"This thing'll blow over," the investigator from the law firm said, "once the media latches on to another story."

Lori spoke again. "You can stay at my lake house."

Kent could see, from searching Caroline's face, that Lori's suggestion didn't sit too well. Nothing sat well with Caroline, and hadn't since that night in her bedroom, a week ago, when he'd done and said everything wrong.

Well, not everything, he amended in his head, glancing at Caroline, who perched on the sofa's end, her arms crossed protectively. Before he'd ruined the mood, they had been good together. Best not to think about that.

But how could he not recall her statements about bad blood? She had accepted him but he held strong doubts that she'd be as willing to look past his heritage.

Doubts didn't stop his dreams. How great it would be to take her into his arms and confess his pathetic secrets, then have her smile and say, "Natalie is enough for me."

It would never happen. Their love affair had "finished" written all over it. All he could do was hang on until the bitter end, praying along the way that some miracle would happen.

His eyes swept over the penthouse great room. Lori Hardwicke occupied a chair, Ted O'Banyon had his arm draped over the back of the sofa, at the opposite end from Caroline.

O'Banyon, hard-boiled and fifty, had a shock of gray hair, and eyeglasses so thick, they gave the impression he could look at anyone under a microscope, which served him well, first as detective with the Dallas Police Department. He gulped a shot of whiskey-over-ice. "Sounds like a good idea, the three of you moving to Lori's place. It's secluded, gated. Security men can stake it out. No reporters will pass the gate or the beach."

"I don't trust your ideas, Mr. O'Banyon." Cutting eyes toward Kent, Caroline included him. "You did a lousy job of keeping that Garrison insect at bay."

Her insult rolled off O'Banyon. "Call me Ted."

"*Ted,* Garrison broke the story this morning. Already newspaper reporters are here. The news channel, too."

"An unfortunate situation." Lori voiced the words Kent wanted to speak, but couldn't, since Caroline wouldn't listen to his explanations. "Kent tried to nip it in the bud. So did Ted. If the Hardwicke Law Firm can't kill a story, no one can."

Caroline gawked at Lori, as if she'd sprouted horns. "And just what did the Hardwicke machine do?"

"Used every legal avenue available." Palms turned

up. "But the First Amendment is on the media's side."

"Lori's right." O'Banyon took another sip. "Kent and I tried the back door, the front being shut. Called in a marker with Garrison's boss at the *Eye*. Didn't work. Story's too hot."

Caroline glared, first at O'Banyon, next at Kent. "The main thing is, your ploys didn't work. And now I've got a baby who needs shelter from gossip and innuendo."

"I've got a library of Mel Gibson movies at the lake," Lori imparted. "I've prompted them all to his nude scenes."

"Really?" Caroline perked up, which irked Kent. "All right, I accept your offer."

Lori smiled; before she could comment, Caroline got solemn again. "Baby can't grow up behind a locked gate. As for now, she has an appointment with her pediatrician. We can't put it off. She may need heart surgery."

Kent cringed. His eyes tried to telegraph a message, begging Lori to keep quiet, but she wasn't looking toward him.

"Heart surgery? Kent! Surely you told her—"

"I think this might be a good time for you and O'Banyon to leave," Kent said. The guests got the picture.

Once the elevator door had closed on them, Caroline advanced on Kent. The hour of reckoning had arrived.

Big-time.

Chapter Eleven

What had been the meaning of Lori's vague statement, the one that prompted Kent's exit shot to her and Ted?

Lately Caroline had suffered disappointments, most centered on a lawyer who talked out of both sides of his mouth, but now, while glaring at him, she figured the worst was yet to come. "Spill it. What else do you have in your bag of tricks?"

"Think I'll check on Gnat Nat."

"Do I need to add coward to your list of traits?"

He reverted to the wet bar and grabbed a soft drink from the refrigerator. He popped the top, and took a swallow. "I am a coward where you're concerned."

"Oh, Kent—what did I ever do to make you distrust me?"

"It's myself I don't trust."

Caroline sighed. Did his problem have something

to do with that old bugaboo, his childhood? She failed to see how today twined with yesterday. Whatever had him snared, she vowed to turn him around.

"We need to clear the air," she said.

"I'd like that."

She considered backtracking to the sofa, but went to the kitchen, wordlessly measuring coffee into the coffeemaker's basket and adding water to the reservoir. Kent collected cups. Once the finished product was ready, she started to sit at the table, but he had a different idea.

"Caro, let's go to the balcony."

Following his lead, she paused long enough to grab the baby monitor. There was a pair of chaise longues on the narrow balcony, facing the city of Dallas, and Kent placed the tray of coffee and cups on the table between them. Caroline sat down.

He took the edge of the other lounger. "Ready for coffee?"

Placing the monitor next to the tray, she leaned back to eye the skyline. "I don't have much of a thirst right now."

I'm hungry for you, darn it! It was probably some sort of sickness, needing him this badly. But every time she looked at him, except when outside influences took her attention, she ogled him like some lovelorn teenager. The sight of his clothed behind recalled how it felt nude, beneath her fingers. One look at his mouth, and she got an itch in her lower parts; they cried out for him. The list was endless. Everything about Kent made her want more. Everything except his attitude. Attitudes could be changed.

"Are you ready to tell me what Lori meant?" she asked.

He took a drink of coffee, then set his cup down with deliberate purpose. "Yesterday, Dr. McBride came by the house, while you were with your executive recruiter."

Her job search ranked low right now. While not commenting on the power of Mackay, getting a doctor to make a house call, she frowned. It deepened as she tried to second-guess the prognosis for Baby, yet... "Lori seemed shocked, a mere mention of heart surgery."

A protracted moment past before Kent said anything. "The pediatrician found nothing wrong with Gnat Nat's heart. Nor with anything else. Apparently she's outgrown the murmur."

"Thank God." Exhaling loudly, Caroline sagged against the cushions. She silently formed a prayer of thanksgiving. Strangely, it now seemed she could tackle anything, now that she knew Baby carried the bloom of health.

"What took you so long to tell me?" she asked.

"You weren't speaking to me last night. Then this morning, well, you know what happened. The reporters."

She understood. "I did turn my back on you."

"And I've kept secrets."

No use arguing that, but it surprised Caroline when he set the table aside and scooted his chair closer to take her hand. "My timing is off, but you need to hear my secrets. Caro, after Don and Ruth died, I requested a copy of Gnat Nat's medical records. It did note a heart murmur. But the doctor advised the Perrys— their baby might grow out of it."

"That's not what you told me." Caroline slipped her fingers from his. "You said she needed surgery."

"No. You drew your own conclusions."

"You didn't correct my misconceptions."

"If I hadn't appealed to your sensitive side, you would've turned her out."

Her vow to be supportive slipped. *I traded one lying man for another.* "Anything to get your way, that's what you do."

"If I hadn't, where would it have left Gnat Nat?"

"She wouldn't be with a gullible sister. And she wouldn't be at the mercies of a lawyer who ought to be brought up on a morals charge."

"Morals charge? For crying out loud, Caro, you need to get your charges straight."

"Make fun of me, you pompous goat! Better I should have gotten my hunk fixes from infomercials, or from Lori's Mel Gibson tapes." Even if it meant starving to death in a fiberglass cast, she should have been more cautious.

"Your regrets hurt me. I'd hoped you could find a place for me in your heart."

"You've messed with my head too often, Kent. You made me love you, then—" What had she admitted!

A smile broke across his face. "You love me?"

"That was a poor choice of words. I'll admit, you were everything I've ever searched for, even when I didn't realize I was looking." Huffing off the lounger, Caroline wanted to kick his shin, but that was beneath her dignity. She boosted her nose instead. As an afterthought she snatched the baby monitor up, then gave the French door a yank. "How can I love you when I can't even respect you?"

Before Caroline could put one foot inside the penthouse, much less collect her cat, a sly tortie shot onto the balcony.

Greezy.

Who could dive-bomb to the ground.

"Grab her, Kent!"

They moved like the Keystone Kops, chasing that stupid cat up and down the balustraded platform. At one point Kent managed to grab Greezy's ribs, but she slipped out of his grip, as if bathed in cooking oil. Thereafter, she leapt to the rail on all fours, hackles raised. Both Caroline and Kent froze.

"Murr-ow!"

"We need to calm down," Kent whispered from the corner of his mouth.

"True. Don't make any fast moves."

"We need bait."

"Salmon Delight," Caroline whispered succinctly.

"I'll get it."

It seemed forever, although it couldn't have been more than a couple of minutes, before Kent returned with an open can of Greezy's favorite food. "Here, kitty, kitty." He clicked his tongue several times. "Hungry?"

Greezy waggled whiskers. Her slanted gaze went from man to woman. She set one paw in front of the other, but rather than alighting her perch, she walked the rail.

Caroline just about had the heart attack that she'd once figured Baby would suffer.

"Hungry?" Kent repeated. "Kitty, kitty. Gree-zy, come here, kitty," he crooned and took a tentative step forward, his palm outstretched and filled with a can of Greezy's standard delight.

"If I ever get my hands on that cat," Caroline muttered through teeth fastened together, "I'll wring her neck."

He inched closer, under Greezy's watchful eye. She extended the neck in jeopardy to sniff the can. But didn't take the bait. Haughty as Cleopatra of the Nile, she started in reverse, daring a move by lower forms of life.

"Get down from there," Caroline ordered in as even a voice as she could muster.

"Murr-ow."

A babyish cry suddenly emitted from the electronic monitor; it startled the cat. She flinched. Teetered. Toward Dallas. Caroline died a thousand deaths.

Kent lunged forward.

Caroline screamed, thinking she'd lose both cat and man. In the same instant she did her own lunging, grabbing Kent by the waistband of his trousers and putting everything she had into tumbling him backward, to safety.

They fell to the balcony floor, the heavy weight of his body knocking the wind from her lungs. A ball of mottled fur went straight up, human fingers—Kent's—attached to the feline. He was not letting go.

Like a star quarterback, he shot from the pile of bodies, twisted and got to his feet in the same motion, then threw a pass straight into the living room.

"Murr-owwww!" whizzed through the air, on a course opposite Dallas.

Her rescuer slammed the French door; two panes cracked.

Another cry emitted from the baby monitor. Natalie.

"Let's get a grip," Caroline said, her voice coming out in puffs. "Baby needs us."

They both made sure the coast was clear of Greezy before opening the door again. Caroline hurried toward the baby's room, but did slow down to hiss at

the venomous cat eyes peeking from behind swordlike
leaves of a dracaena. "You're a marked cat."

"Murr-ow?"

By the time Caroline reached Baby's room, she no-
ticed something peculiar. Natalie wasn't crying. In fact
she had an arm around a teddy bear, her diapered behind in the air, her legs tucked under. She slept. Peacefully, calmly. This was the first time she'd gone back
to sleep without the tools of love.

This was indeed a good night, despite the horrors
of it.

All of a sudden, it deflated, the balloon of anxieties
about Baby. No heart trouble. And Natalie felt safe.
So relieved was Caroline, her feet couldn't hold her
weight.

But manly hands swept her up.

She roped arms around Kent's neck and let him
carry her to her room. He laid her on the bed, before
shifting to sit on the edge of it. Her pent-up tears fell,
both in relief and frustration.

"Don't cry," he whispered and levered down to
brush her cheek with a fingertip. "Everything's going
to be all right."

Hang frustrations. She didn't want to think about
the many things that separated them. What she wanted
was a few tender mercies. And he gave them. He
stretched out to stroke her spine and to kiss away tears.

"I could have lost you," she sobbed, loving the
brush of his mustache and hating the mere idea that it
could have been squashed on the sidewalk. "And
Greezy. I'm going to wring that c-cat's neck. I have
every right. She's incorrigible!"

"She is. Too much of a heritage stew, that one.
We're all a product of our kind, so don't think ill of

her for it. She's an American, just like you and me. A stew of heredity.''

''I'm English and Cherokee—not the vehicular variety.''

''Aren't you the one, knowing your lineage.''

''Kent, did that sound pompous?'' Caroline asked, recalling his nebulous background. ''I didn't mean it to.''

''You stated a fact, as you understand it. But we were talking about Greezy. You won't do her bodily harm. Whenever she deigns to forgive you for saving her hide, you'll pet her and hug her and tell her you're pleased she didn't fall. Just like I want you to do with me.''

''I am glad you didn't fall.''

Having come close to losing him, Caroline put everything into perspective. Yes, he'd lied to her, but unlike Frank, he didn't do it for his own benefit.

''You mean so much to me,'' she whispered.

He kissed her again, this time as a lover. Their bodies melted together. They touched, as she'd known each wanted to touch the other. Caressing, stroking, squeezing in that natural way of lovers eternal, when they have been to the edge and had the luck to return from it.

''Caro,'' he whispered, once they were devoid of material barriers to their yearning flesh. His hand swept over her derriere, cupping it. ''We can't do this unprotected.''

''Actually, I've been to the doctor myself. He wrote a prescription.''

''That's...that's wise.''

''It's simply prudent. I may be naive about many things, but I'm not stupid enough to think we can live together, this heat between us, without something happening. I chose not to replay that night we…''

"I don't want a replay of it, either." He cuddled her, and she felt relief in his muscles. "Thank you for taking precautions, Caro. They're smart."

Greezy selected that moment to flounce into the bedroom and hop on the bed, atop Kent's shoulder. The tone of her murr-ow had the pitch of forgiveness.

Now was the time Caroline could exact punishment, yet she smiled and tucked a purring cat between woman and man. She even planted a kiss on the top of a head with scant room for a brain. "Sweetie…"

"I think I've been replaced in your affections by a cat."

"No way." Caroline nestled against Kent's shoulder, the heavy pelt of his chest hair tickling her nose. Greezy, exhausted, fell asleep in the V of their bodies. "I want you like the dickens, Mackay. But things happen for a reason, even something as minor as a cat's interruption. We shouldn't get too caught up in our relationship. Like I said, like you said some days back, things happen. Condoms break, pills fail. I don't want to be pushed into a shotgun wedding any more than you do. Nor would I want my child to grow up, having a father who doesn't want him. Her.''

"You've got a point."

Caroline foresaw a future that could be part roses, part pigweed. "You and I have a tie that binds, from here on out. For Baby's sake as well as our own, we shouldn't take chances."

"If that's what you want." He didn't leave her bed. Nor did he remove her from the cat-filled cradle of his arms. But he did say, "You said you love me. Okay, you qualified it, but you said it. I make my own choices, too. And I prefer to believe you love me.''

"True love has no qualifiers. And you've manipulated me from the beginning.'' On a further wing of self-preservation, Caroline said, "I love skylines and sunsets and rain showers. And I love myself too much to settle for anything less than my dreams.''

"What exactly are your dreams now?'' he asked guardedly.

"I don't think I should answer that. I don't know how you feel about me, truly feel about me.'' It was more than beneath her dignity, digging for an avowal, but if he didn't see a future for them, she needed to change his outlook.

He didn't disappoint. "I love you. I think I fell in love the night you kissed me beneath my mustache.''

His tender words seeped into her heart, making it surge. "Kent, I admit, I love you. You mean more than sunsets or skylines or rain showers. But I need to trust you.''

"I pray you'll forgive me. And that you'll learn to accept me as I am. As flawed as the day I came into this world.''

"I'll try,'' she promised.

Again they kissed, but getting squashed between lovers sent Greezy into a yowl that pitched her from the lair. The cat traipsed out of the bedroom. "Murrow,'' echoed from the hallway.

"She's PMSing again,'' Caroline commented.

"It is difficult, keeping you ladies happy.'' He framed her face with his palms, his thumbs holding her steady so that her gaze couldn't waver from his. "I want to make you happy. Will you forgive me for lying about Gnat Nat?''

"I'm working on it," she said honestly.

"If there's a chance for us, I'll count myself lucky." A moment lapsed. "Caro, there are things you don't know about me. I love you, but I'm not ready to talk. Can you bear with me?"

Curiosity was killing her, yet she banked it. "Provided it's not something like you're an ax murderer. Or that you're in collusion with subversive groups to overthrow the government." She wasn't teasing when she said, "I wouldn't like the idea of finding out you've had a vasectomy, although it's a given you haven't."

"Why is my potency an issue?" he asked.

"Maybe it's not. If this love of ours goes nowhere, then it's a moot issue. But if I ever love enough, and if I'm ever loved enough, to give marriage another try, I do want children."

Kent needed a cigarette. He hadn't smoked one in ten years, had thought the craving behind him. One thing he didn't crave was sex.

Ax murderer, she'd mentioned. Did the sins of the father rest on the son's shoulders? They did in Kent's case.

And Caroline wanted kids.

There was no getting around it.

Somehow, here in her bedroom, ensconced in her bed, her admission about wanting to be a mother ringing in his ears, he found a voice. "You ought to have babies." *Not mine.* So where did that leave them? In love and without a chance for happiness. The issue of children would always come between them. *You'll have to let her go. Let her find someone else to love. Someone who'll want to father her children.*

Could he let her go?

He'd have to.

Unless he could change her mind. How fair was that? Fair, be damned. He wouldn't let go. The mere idea of some schmuck knowing the secrets of her lush body gave him the creeps.

He plumped his pillow. "Let's talk this through. Say you did get married and got pr-pregnant. What about your career?"

"What's that got to do with anything?"

"Most companies have maternity-leave policies, but let's shoot from the hip. Too many corporations are still stranded in the sixties, in the Good Old Boy network. When it comes to promotions and whatnot, those guys work around the law. They find excuses not to promote when they think a woman's going to take maternity leave every few years. Maternity leave, and time off when their kids are sick."

"You think so, Kent?"

"I know so. I won a case like that, a couple years ago."

It was underhanded, kneading the clay of her emotions, but he spoke the truth. Besides, he had an idea rolling that would settle the issue of her career, once and for all. Telling her about the concept wasn't timely, since he hadn't worked out the particulars.

He further explained, "I rep'd the employer. A female employee sued. She'd been passed over for a promotion, basically for staying home too often with her sick kids."

"If Baby's sick, I'm not leaving her to a sitter or an au pair or a nanny or any one else."

"I know you won't." It was wicked of him, being

gladdened by the direction their conversation had taken, but wasn't this what he needed?

"Kent, what are we going to do about Baby?"

He strove for a lighter mood. "Well, we could par-boil her, or can her. But I prefer to snuggle Gnat Nat."

"Oh, you silly goose. I mean, what are we going to do about Baby and our present problem. The *Enquiring Eye?*"

Before Greezy's tightrope act, even after he'd been exposed on the heart-condition issue, Caroline hadn't wanted his advice. That she still spoke to a callous liar, and sought his counsel, heartened him.

He answered her question. "We shouldn't run like whipped dogs to Lori's lake house. Gnat Nat's too young to read newspapers. And, like O'Banyon said, this'll die down as soon as people rubberneck the next sensational story."

"Yes, but, someday she'll find out about her unique story."

"And we'll be the ones to tell her."

"I'm trying to picture our tomorrows, but they're too vague," Caroline said, echoing his thoughts. "I suppose we'll have to play it by ear. But, Kent, what if Baby—" a shudder "—fell off your balcony?"

"We need to find a new place to live."

"Kent! As soon as the custody thing goes through, I must move into my own house."

That idea went down his gullet like a medicine ball. "Will you promise me something?" he asked, needing to buy time.

"What?" That single word came hesitantly.

"You won't move until after the hearing."

"What about the balcony?"

"That, Caro, I can do something about. Right now."

Kent was an enigma, for sure. Beyond the obvious, what had he meant? *I can do something.* Curiosity got the better of Caroline, somewhere in the dead of night, so she crept from the bedroom to find where he'd gone. She found him, stretched out on a pallet, sleeping, blocking the door to the balcony.

Natalie wouldn't be able to pass him.

How could Caroline get past his aversion to children? How could she be certain whether it was fatherhood that scared him the most, or plain old marriage?

He would open up someday, would tell her what was amiss, and she'd patiently await that forthrightness. Rome wasn't built in a day.

She returned to her bedroom and slept restfully, but awoke to the incessant sounds of a hammer striking, over and over and over again.

"Why is that door hammered shut?" Angie Cortez poured cooked oatmeal into a bowl. "And why are the panes broken?"

"Kent and I don't want Baby to fall off the balcony." Caroline collected the oatmeal and blew steam from it. Feeling calm and serene, despite the reporters who were hovering downstairs, she smiled, first at the nanny, last at the little girl seated in a high chair. "I hadn't even thought about that dangerous balcony. Not until Greezy almost fell."

"Greezy isn't happy." Angie poured orange juice into a sipper cup and handed it to Natalie. "Those cats that look like grease rags, they don't like to be cooped up.''

"'O?''

"What, darling?" Caroline turned her attention to Baby.

"Kiss?"

"Oh, yes. Another kiss would be nice.'' Nothing was better than starting the morning off with a kiss from Natalie, unless it would be a few from her attorney. Caroline and Kent had shared a tender one, before he'd left for work. She pressed her lips to Baby's soft cheek, and gave thanks that fate had brought them together. The three of them. Hopefully forever.

"Why don't you give Greezy to me?" Angie asked. "Tomas and I have many cats. We have a big yard with a fence, where our cats can't get out.''

"Give Greezy away? Oh, Angie, I can't. I love her.''

"She is unhappy here.''

"Kit cat. Baby 'uvs kit cat.''

"Did you hear that? Baby said a whole sentence. Angie, she's really talking! Oh, Baby, I love you!'' Caroline got Natalie out of the high chair, quickly. Dancing her around and around in the kitchen, she nuzzled, kissed and bragged profusely.

At the end of her display, Caroline glanced at Angie, who had a brow hiked upward. "Thanks but no thanks, Angie. I can't let you take Greezy. She's too important to Baby and me.''

Thankfully, to Caroline's amazement, the cat settled down. She took to her condo, like a tragic figure might take to her bed. Greezy made her daily exits at mealtimes, usually with hisses of disapproval, then returned to her square of the penthouse to pout.

The real trouble lay in the lack of household harmony.

Kent kept busy at the office, arriving home late each evening, his arms filled with groceries and supplies. Too late for dinner, and too late for Caroline. She was exhausted, come bedtime. The covey of reporters kept their vigil, the penthouse under siege. That necessitated keeping Natalie indoors, even though the toddler longed to be in the sun and with the ducks.

Both Caroline and Angie devised ways to entertain. Unfortunately, the nanny got high blood pressure; a doctor ordered her to bed at home. Caroline missed the woman's presence. Her smiling, pleasant self. And her help.

Running after a toddler was no simple task.

One evening, Lori Hardwicke called at the penthouse. She proceeded to get down on all fours for a game of chase, then engaged in a ticklefest culminating into a round of giggles from both participants, when Lori blew raspberries on Baby's tummy. Caroline joined in the laughter, mainly at the comical sight of the perfectly turned-out Lawyer Lady with mussed hair and runs in her Neiman-Marcus hose.

Of course, Caroline's job search had to be shelved during this period. Another week passed before the reporters packed up and went away, chasing other people's curiosity appeal. Two days later, Caroline dared set foot outside the building. How lovely it was, breathing fresh air and standing on terra firma. She understood Greezy's pursuit of freedom.

Eventually things got even brighter. Angie returned.

The executive recruiter telephoned. "I have an interview lined up for you, with a small oil company here in Dallas. Could you see the man on Friday?"

What a question. "I'll be there."

Friday, she dressed with care, nerves on end. She needed a job, but hated the idea of leaving Baby from nine to five. "Other women have done it," she told Kent that morning, when he turned the elevator key to leave for the office. "So can I."

"That's the spirit, sweetheart. But if the interview doesn't work out, I've got something up my sleeve that might interest you."

The elevator doors opened, they stepped inside and Caroline tweaked his mustache. "So you say, Mackay."

"This touching yet not touching is more than I can take," he admitted and backed her into the corner. "I'm tired of being careful. You know I'm a heel and a jerk, but I've got a hunger that won't go away. Feed me, woman."

"But we agreed not to—"

"Caro, have you been taking your pills?" At her nod, Kent curved a hand around her waist. "Couldn't we once just forget about everything but us? Just once." Eyes half-lidded, he asked, "Shall we go back upstairs?"

Chapter Twelve

Temptation. That was Kent and his offer in the elevator. The brass doors rolled open, as if Moses had parted the Red Sea. Outside the lobby, the promised land of employment waited. Inside, upstairs, pleasure beckoned. But hadn't Caroline been the one to chisel the commandments in stone?

Thus, she glanced at her wristwatch. "I really mustn't miss my appointment."

Kent darted his tongue to her ear. "Last chance. Go. Or come with me."

"I—I'll have to think about your offer."

She stepped into the lobby, out the building's entrance and into her Festiva for the drive to J-Bar Petroleum. Along the way she made up her mind. She wanted Kent Mackay, and if it meant breaking her own rule, so what? They were lovers already; she was armed against pushing him into something he didn't want. And how far had she gotten in her campaign to turn him around, by going the punishment-through-denial route?

But it was too late to return to the penthouse.

She parked the clunker in the J-Bar Petroleum lot.

Five minutes into her appointment with Stan Mallory, Caroline knew she had an interview with a vampire. It hadn't begun that way, when the youngish fellow with a shock of red hair scanned her résumé and had pointed out the obvious, that her experience warranted only an entry-level position.

"I don't expect a top slot on the organizational chart, sir." Caroline arranged her hands primly in her lap and met Mallory's gaze. "I would appreciate a chance to prove my worth."

His forefinger scratched behind an ear. "I get a weird feeling, as if I ought to know you. Wait." He went owl-eyed. "You're the girl with the little sister. You know, the test-tube baby with a mother old enough to be her great-granny."

"I'm not a girl, Mr. Mallory," she said lamely, knowing she shouldn't out and out lie to the man who might hire her.

"What's her name? Natasha, isn't it? Didn't she inherit twenty-million bucks?"

Actually it was closer to ten, but Caroline had no intention of correcting him. She slipped fingers around her purse; working for J-Bar had lost its appeal.

He pushed an intercom button. "Haul your big hair this way, Merry sugar. There's someone you'll want to meet."

Caroline's lips flattened. Where did this jackass hide his copies of *Sluts in Cyberspace*?

Before the fair-haired secretary entered Mallory's

office, the interviewee surged to stand. "I'm outta here."

"You don't seem too upset by what happened," Kent said over an impromptu late dinner, the first evening he'd dared to arrive at the penthouse before midnight. The blues from a CD drifted through the great room, soft lights surrounding the woman Kent loved.

"I'm not upset," she replied. "It wasn't meant to be."

From her tone and general attitude, he believed Caroline. And he stared, just stared. Lodged on the sofa, dressed in shorts and a T-shirt, her bare feet tucked beneath just-plump-enough legs, she had done with her usual ponytail. His fingers, as if they had minds of their own, called out, begging to touch the luxurious mass.

He didn't move. Wouldn't move.

She shifted her weight, a carton of moo goo gai pan in one hand, a fork in the other. He couldn't help studying a slender ankle exposed for a moment by that shift of hers, and he recalled how it felt to slide his tongue up and down it. Damn.

Her good behavior carried on. "I'm glad I found out about Mallory's personality before I got on the payroll."

Actually, Kent was glad the interview had soured. If not, the ideas he planned to propose might not rest on eager ears.

Ideas? They fled, replaced by thoughts of how much he yearned for her, how he wanted to sleep with arms around her at night and wake up each morning, Caroline still there. But! If she equated him with felonious trash, she might dump him like so much refuse.

The fingers that ached to caress Caroline? They stuck chopsticks in shrimp-fried rice. "How would you like to shift gears? Do something outside the petroleum industry?"

"Like what?"

"How about with a company called Easy Access?"

"Tell me about it."

"It's nonprofit. A center that locates folks in need, puts them in touch with various aid foundations. Easy Access even provides financial help, when necessary. Physical help, too. Whatever needs to be done."

"What a wonderful organization," she enthused, setting the white carton down. "But they'll want a social worker, or someone trained along those lines."

"No, they won't." It was all he could do to contain a smirk. "You might say I have easy access to the big shot at Easy Access."

"Did you pull one of your deals?" Caroline imparted a sharp look. "Did you put in a good word for me to call in a marker or something?"

"Not in the least."

That seemed to placate her. Tigress eyes on him, she said, "I can't imagine what sort of contribution I could make."

"You'll administer Easy Access and oversee fundraising."

"Kent Mackay, I'm not slick enough for such a job."

"What about those spaghetti suppers and garage sales you put together for that Pasadena shelter? Hey, stop with the sad-sack face. You can handle Easy Access. As for your specialty, you've got empathy on your side. You know what it's like to be tied to a wheelchair. You could make a difference."

"Kent, you're very kind. But I do believe you're prejudiced. You're imagining I could hold down that position, but empathy isn't enough. I have no training, nothing to recommend me along those lines. Suppers and selling junk won't cut it, not to buy expensive services and medical equipment."

"Don't worry—you'll be in touch with charity circles. Lori's contacts are top-shelf. You'll do fine."

Caroline appeared like a child disappointed at Christmas. "I doubt the director at Easy Access, or whatever you call the person in charge, will feel the same way."

"You're very wrong." Despite the sagacious part of his brain that said "hands off," Kent cruised down the sofa and pulled her onto his lap. "It's your show. You make the calls. When you're not too busy, you can even take Gnat Nat to work with you. Do whatever you please. *You* are the executive director."

"Excuse me?" Caroline drew back, more than wary. "What have you done?"

"I've funded the organization for the first three years." It took a chunk from his investment portfolio, but why worry? There was always another corporation like Snappy Sours to bill. And the tax man would get zilch for a while. "I signed the papers this morning. I want you to direct Easy Access."

"That's charity."

He slid fingers into her hair. "Is there a more noble cause?"

With Kent's fingers caressing her scalp, Caroline made the effort to think clearly. Even though she longed to stay in his lap and needed to be there, music playing, the lights soft, it offended her, that he would create a career for her. As if she couldn't find a place in the sun on her own.

Get real, girl. He is your place in the sun.

His thumb stroked her bottom lip, as he asked, "What's it going to be? Will you accept my offer?"

It would be downright selfish to refuse. There were people in bad straits who needed his generosity, and Caroline was eager to add the elbow grease. Furthermore, she'd have the chance to repay all those San Antonio kindnesses.

"I accept."

"Thank you," he whispered.

For a stretch of moments they gazed at each other, and the elation she felt spilled into action. "Shall we seal this with a kiss, noble benefactor?"

Fingers behind her neck, he pulled her to him, as if for a kiss, yet lips hovered beneath hers. "You said we shouldn't do this. I'll stand up, go to my room, whatever."

It wasn't easy, admitting she was ready to forget her own rules. Better he should think it his idea. She inched off his lap and down the sofa, lay back and boosted her feet to his thighs. "I asked for a kiss, not more," she lied.

"Why don't I grant your wish?" He lifted one ankle to his lips, brushing that mink-soft mustache along her sensitive skin. "There. Done."

The rogue had the nerve to replace her foot in his lap, his *expanding* lap.

"That's not nice, teasing my ankle, then quitting."

"Just playing by your rules." His bedroom blues had a glint in them. "Of course, turnabout is fair play. I kissed your ankle. You ought to give something in return. It wouldn't be breaking the rules, if I just rubbed around the outside of your sweet little place for a minute or two, would it?''

She could go for more than a minute or two. ''What guarantee would I have? You might break the rules.''

Two fingers went to his forehead, in a scout's salute. ''On my honor, I wouldn't. I do want your respect.''

She feared he'd do that very thing and leave them both worse off than they already were. If anyone had to give, it must be her. ''Say you were to go too far. Say you couldn't stop.'' She angled to her knees and canted toward him; it was no accident that the side of her breast brushed his arm. ''What if I didn't object? What if I promise to still respect you in the morning?''

''I'd say you're in for a very long night, chick.''

''Prove it.''

Their chuckles melted into one, before they got serious. His mouth met hers, and their leashed desires went wild.

In joyous celebration he helped her from her clothes; she did the same for him. He thereafter cherished her, as if she were an icon. It wasn't the high jinks of wild lovemaking. It was the coming together of two people who desperately longed for the succor of the other.

It was supremely satisfying.

And when it was over, they cuddled on the leather sofa, her back to the cushions. Her eyes closed. She luxuriated in Kent and the way he touched her heart, bodily and spiritually. Bless him. Right then, everything seemed rosy.

Her body still thrumming, she considered the whole picture. ''What a dream you are,'' she stated, thinking about his appeal, both of the flesh and as a philanthropist.

"I do aim to please."

"I'm going to devote a lot of time to this," she said, thinking about Easy Access and closing her eyes on the concepts that formed in her head. "Oh, yes. Mmm."

"Sounds good."

"I hope I don't drain your resources."

"I'll do my best to make more."

"I suppose I'll have to start off easy."

She felt his head shake as he said, "No need for that. I'm up to fast."

"It's going to take a lot of money," she worried.

He pulled her hip toward him. "What for?"

"The least of which, I need to be paid."

"Paid!" He pitched halfway from their sofa nest. "What do you mean paid?"

She opened her eyes to a shocked mien. "I don't intend to do this for nothing."

"What are you talking about?"

"Kent, surely you don't expect me to work for nothing. I'll have to have a salary."

White as a piece of paper, he got in her face. "Let's get this straight. You want me to pay for services rendered?"

Realization plugged in. She blushed. "Good heavens, Kent, I was talking about Easy Access."

A chuckle heaved his shoulders, vibrating from his body to hers. "You scared the hell out of me, Caro."

"How awful of me, thinking about Easy Access, when I'm still in your arms."

"Aw, now, my little tigress, don't fret. I know you're excited about your new career. As long as you stay excited about me, I'm willing to share your favors."

"Tigress? I'm not a tigress. I'm just a woman from Pasadena, probably out of my element. But trying to fit in."

"Keep trying, cat woman. How 'bout a drink?" He craned his neck up. "Or should we finish our dinner?"

"Fix us a drink, noble one."

Kent, in his birthday suit, strode toward the wet bar, while Caroline took a long moment to stare at his well-formed behind. He not only aimed to please, he pleased.

This was a night for true confessions.

In the dark of midnight, her head sheltered next to Kent's shoulder, Caroline listened to Kent admit, "I'm not really too crazy about your cat."

"That's because she comes out of her condo only to eat or to nap on your bed. Then you have to pay the cleaning people an extra two bucks a day to change your linens."

"Yeah, right. I really worry about an extra two hundred cents a day." He rolled back his eyes. "Really, Caro, I don't know what you see in Greezy."

"Companionship. She came into my life when I was so alone and lonely that I took up her companionship like a sponge. The same week I left Frank, I pulled into a convenience-store parking lot. Two little girls were giving away kittens. I took the ugliest one."

"Greezy isn't ugly," Kent defended, despite his professed dislike. "She's got fine lines and aristocratic features."

"And an iffy bloodline. I wonder what happens, mixing up a Siamese and no-telling-what that makes for a cat like Greezy? They're so high-strung, torties. There isn't a thing symmetrical about that girl's coat.

You'd think there would be, her mother being a prize. Genes can sure get messed up.''

Was Caroline imagining it, or did Kent suddenly go too still?

If he did, he recovered enough to squeeze her elbow gently. "You love her, despite her flaws," he said. "That's the main thing."

"I must admit, early on, I would study her for the longest, trying not to be put off by her sheer ugly fur."

"Then you never really accepted her, as is."

It hit Caroline, like a slap of cold water. He was making a correlation between his own flaws and a mottled cat's. While she'd been sticking a foot in her mouth. She cringed inwardly, trying to cover her blunder. "I accept Greezy. I love her. She may be weird, but she was mine. Shoot, no one is perfect. Who'd want a perfect person?"

"You're speaking of me, aren't you?" he said slowly.

"If you want to put yourself there, yes."

"It's time I did." He rested his head against the pillows, sliding a wrist beneath his neck to further prop himself up. "Aw, hell, Caro. Enough of my angst. Bright and early, I'm showing you the space I've rented for Easy Access."

"I always have time for your 'angst.'"

She might as well have talked to the wall. Kent refused to say another word on the subject and that did nothing but make her fret. "Kent Mackay, if this has something to do with that cleft palate you used to have, we need to talk. Because I thought we got past that, back in July."

"Caro, go to sleep."

Aggravating man!

* * *

Kent had been skirting around his stand on fathering children. Today he and Caroline visited the empty offices set aside for Easy Access, near Parkland Hospital. It was time for honesty.

He led her into the storefront quarters, furnished solely with a card table and two folding chairs, and gave brief thought to the time he'd said something about having no wish to become a storefront lawyer. He still didn't want to give up his practice. But he took comfort in knowing part of his earnings would always be diverted for the good of mankind.

Her color high with excitement, Caroline, a shoulder-strap purse swinging as she went, rushed through the three rooms, waxing enthusiastic, even going on about the toilet facilities. It didn't take much to put a bloom on Caroline's face.

"This is going to be marvelous," she chattered, patting a handrail twice. "Isn't it lovely?"

Uninterested in debating the beauties of bathrooms, he retreated to the main part of the suite, Caroline following him, as he said, "Hope you don't mind, I've called an office-furniture store. They're going to fill these rooms."

"Cancel the order. I can get furnishings in boxes. Won't take anytime to put it together. You can help. I'll show you how to use a screwdriver properly. There's something to be said for sharing a project, you know. We could have fun...."

He glowered at her bright face. His hands would never wield a screwdriver, never by choice. "My job is to provide funds, not to make furniture."

"All right. I give. But I trust you didn't pay too

much for desks and such. We shouldn't spend a penny more than necessary on administration.''

''Caro, you are well funded. Don't get parsimonious.''

''Whatever you say.''

She brushed something from her bodice, her action catching his attention. His gaze welded to her bosom. Those were a fine pair, hers, heavy in his hands, their cinnamon tips just right....

She flitted off, bubbling again, unmindful of his licentious regard. ''We will need to hire good counselors. At least one or two. We should seek out the physically challenged.''

''You shouldn't discriminate against them, nor should you be prejudiced against the physically fit. Find the best people.''

''By the way, we didn't discuss my salary.''

Kent grinned. ''All the beans you can eat and four big ones a month.''

''Four thousand dollars?'' Her mouth dropped.

''Four hundred.''

''You slime! That's what you make in an hour.''

He ducked, but not before she elevated her arm to whap his biceps with her purse. ''Okay, Caro. Five big ones.''

She got solemn. ''Baby and I can't live on that.''

''No sense of humor at all, that's you. You're so easy to tease.'' He tossed the shoulder bag to the floor and tickled her ear. ''You're the analyst, Caro. You figure out your salary requirements, and you've got it.''

''I'll be frugal.''

''Don't go overboard with thriftiness.'' He took her

elbows, drawing her to him. "Especially not in your attentions to me. Want to..." He wiggled his brows.

"Kent!" Her eyes went wide, the skin above her white collar flushing. "You don't mean to do some sort of christening ceremony, do you? This is hallowed ground."

"Okay. I won't make sacrilege," he replied and let her go.

"Then let's make talk." Caroline's eyes held a knowing look. "What about last night?"

She'd been waiting for an explanation, he knew darn well. Not quite up to jumping into it, he said, "I never fully explained myself. It's not so much that I dislike your cat, I just think she's never going to be happy in the penthouse."

He thought she spoke a non sequitur, asking, "When is that custody hearing?"

"October fifteenth."

"I must move out. For Greezy's sake. For Natalie's."

"Caro, we've been through this before."

"Won't the judge see me in a better light, if I've got my own household? I know this is the *fin de siècle*, as someone like Lori would say, but don't morals count at all? We're living in what my father called sin."

How could anything so right be sinful? He'd built a foundation on sand, for one.

"Let's talk Texas Code," he suggested. "I'm temporarily in charge of Gnat Nat. No problem there. A guardian shouldn't be incapacitated. We're not. Nor party to a lawsuit concerning or affecting the proposed ward. We're not. We're not indebted to Natalie, except in matters of the heart. Do we lack experience, education or have other good reasons not to be her care-takers? Absolutely not. I think we do a pretty good job of controlling her, and—"

"I'm better at controlling her than you are," Caroline broke in.

"I concede that point."

"Is there anything else?"

"Are you 'notoriously bad'?"

"Kent! I thought you were talking Texas Code."

"The wording is 'Persons whose conduct is notoriously bad.' Granted, the lawmakers weren't word-smiths."

Caroline leveled her gaze with his. "Mind if I ask you something? What if I want to adopt her? Is it within the realm of possibility? You know, she's got all that money."

"Adoption is tricky, Gnat Nat being an heiress. But it can be done. I can get the papers together. If that's what you truly want."

"I want her." Caroline plumbed her spine; her expression had never been more serious. "I want to be her mother. Do this for me, Kent."

He nodded, willing to do almost anything to make her happy.

But tension knotted in his neck. With Caroline, it always came back to motherhood. "Is there any chance you could be satisfied, stopping at one child?" he asked with bated breath.

"Not a chance. Since I was seventeen, I've wanted to bear a child. I put that dream aside awhile, but it's still there, stronger than ever." Her forefinger waved from one end of Easy Access to the other. "It's even more important than this."

His harbored hopes dissolved, creating a void, an

absolute nothing where his shaky prospects had been, leaving despair. There was no need to delve into the deepest of his secrets.

For what he had to say, no empty office would do. "You hungry?" His voice sounded far away to him, the mere concept of food as remote as his voice. "There's a restaurant close by."

"Lunch would be nice."

Thus, they removed to Chez Goyette, Dallas's best small restaurant. The maître d' showed them to an alcove, and over a bottle of excellent French wine, canned violins playing, they waited for their food. Suddenly a romantic setting seemed the worst place to be.

"Caro, you deserve to have kids. But not with me. I'm not interested in raising a family."

The wineglass in her hand got set on the table. A thumb traced the glass's bottom. Slumping back against her chair, she glanced at him, and he'd never seen such hurt in her eyes, not when she'd been disabled and had a little sister dropped in her lap. Not when she'd been scammed at Fill-Er-Fast.

For another moment she grappled for something to say. "What are *you* interested in?"

His lungs refused to work. He owed her a straightforward gaze; he gave it. "All I'm prepared to offer is Easy Access."

A knife of pain slammed through his chest, even before he finished those hurtful words. He hurt for himself. And for Caroline.

"That's too bad," she said, her voice breaking. "I want kids. You don't. But I wish I understood why you don't."

"Like your mother wasn't meant to be one, I'm not meant to be a father."

"That is the most ridiculous thing I've ever heard."

It angered him, her scoff. He'd lived with his own private hell for thirty years, yet she put it down. "Dammit, Caro. I've never asked you to marry me, so why are you uptight about kids?"

"You brought it up. And you're the one who's uptight."

Rising slowly to her feet, she arranged her napkin on a plate and pivoted to the side with military precision. "Please excuse me."

She marched toward the maître d'. "Can you get me a cab—right away?" He nodded and she was out the door.

It would be better to let her go, to allow her to deal with this in her usual way, by licking her wounds in private. But Kent plunked money on the table and rushed to the street.

"Caro, wait!"

The maître d' was whistling, snapping his fingers. Caroline stepped into a taxi that seemed to materialize out of thin air, as if this were New York instead of Texas. Slamming the door, she moved her lips, obviously clicking off instructions to the cabbie. Wheels burned rubber as they left the curb.

With the skewed reasoning of a frantic man, Kent tried to outrun the taxi, but it disappeared from his sight three blocks later. His feet stopped, his shoulders slumping. *You made your bed, Mackay. Now you've gotta lie in it.*

He trudged back to the Cherokee. By the time he reached it, he'd come to another conclusion. He'd given her Easy Access; now he must make her other dream come true.

He drove to the office, drafted adoption papers and stuck them in his briefcase with the intention of taking them to her. While there, he would tell Caroline exactly why marriage wasn't right for them. He didn't look forward to it.

As he made his way toward the exit, Lori rushed toward him. "There's trouble in Houston."

He was a coward, just as Caro had accused. Kent found himself relieved, eager to face whatever trouble didn't have Caroline's name attached to it.

Chapter Thirteen

Running from an argument never settled one. Less than ten minutes after she'd flounced out of Chez Goyette, Caroline regretted leaving Kent to eat burned rubber. She should have stayed, stood her ground and pointed out the truth. He'd lied.

Never was a man more cut out for fatherhood and marriage.

Too bad Caroline didn't get the opportunity to make her big speech. At six that evening, when she expected Kent to pass between the elevator doors, a clerk from the Hardwicke Law Firm presented himself at the penthouse, attaché case in hand.

It held a draft of adoption papers. Kent was making good on his word to win Natalie for her, forever.

"I have to take the papers back," the young man said.

"If you don't mind, I'd like to hold on to them, until after I've talked with Mr. Mackay."

"That could be a good while, ma'am. He's gone to Houston. A cargo ship ran aground in the ship channel. The *Lisle Lady* belongs to one of our clients."

Such a situation warranted his presence, but he went without a change of clothes?

The clerk left, adoption papers in hand.

Natalie toddled into the living room, tugging on Caroline's skirt. "Kenn? Baby want Kenn."

"So does Mommy."

"Mommy?"

Caroline took the puzzled child into her arms and cuddled her. "'O is your mommy."

"Mommy." Once they reached the kitchen, where Angie had left a plate of chicken burritos, Natalie repeated, "Baby want Kenn."

"He had to go away." Caroline cut a tortilla filled with chicken, beans and rice into biteable pieces and handed over a curved-handle fork, designed for a small child. "He'll be back."

"When?" Natalie asked, clear as a bell.

"Soon."

"What 'oon?"

Caroline didn't have an answer. Certainly, he'd left a strong message—soon wouldn't be too soon. "Eat your dinner."

What more could she do? What should she do? Be here waiting for him when he returned? Why not go to the horse's mouth, as her dad had often said?

While Natalie used her fingers to shove burrito into her rosebud mouth, Caroline punched Kent's cellular number. He kept his phone on at all times, she knew.

"Your call cannot be completed at this time," a

voice droned. "The customer you have dialed has turned the mobile unit off...."

"Great."

What next? She could pack, leave the keys to Easy Access, then decamp. But she stalled.

The next day Kent did send word, in a roundabout way, by telephoning Angie, saying he'd be gone for several days. Caroline would wait. She wouldn't give up on Kent Mackay.

A lot could be accomplished in a few days, even by a woman toiling with a heart that ran on three cylinders.

Easy Access moved along. Caroline refused the expensive furniture and ordered used, then arranged it; the telephones and office machines were installed; she interviewed a score of secretaries, social workers and health-care professionals. She contacted a high school. The counselor put her in touch with two students in wheelchairs who were interested in trading off mornings and afternoons, manning the phones.

That evening, just as Caroline began to collect her purse and lock the office, Lori Hardwicke swept into Easy Access, the scent of French perfume accompanying her, while she carried a bouquet of roses with a bow tied around its vase.

Flowers placed on a desk, she dusted her hands. "A token to express my best wishes."

It was good to see Lori, and best wishes were more than needed, those blood-red buds recalling...well, it was best not to remember.

The woman sat on the sofa.

"What do you think about this?" The lady lawyer crossed her long, shapely legs at the knee. "I'd like to give a dinner to introduce Easy Access to society. And to—'' a conspiratorial wink ''—drum up contributions. How does November first sound?''

''Marvelous,'' Caroline replied, enthusiastic.

''I'll mark my calendar. Tell me, have you given any thought to contracting with a professional fundraiser? I can recommend a few.''

Eager for anything that would benefit the organization, Caroline agreed. The women chatted for several minutes, going over long-range plans for Easy Access, but the rap session took a personal turn when Lori said, ''You cannot imagine how it delights me, seeing Kent keen on this project.''

What excited him at the moment? Did he ever think of home, or Natalie? Or Caroline? She said, ''He's worked very hard to please me.''

''You're a lucky woman.''

''Obviously you think he's grand. Why didn't you ever want him for your own?''

Lori smoothed an upswept hairdo that didn't need smoothing. ''He's just too touchy about his mouth.''

So there it was. Caroline's conclusions hadn't been wrong, although not a clue on how to deal with it came to mind.

''I have two requirements in a lover—confidence being the first,'' Lori admitted. ''I thought Kent had it—I would've never hired him if I hadn't—but I spend a lot of time being a sister of sorts to him.''

Caroline couldn't stop the frisson of jealousy that reared up. Apparently Kent had confided in Lori, when he had a zipper on his mouth in *his* lover's presence. Oh, stop it, she ordered herself. It was great that Kent had a friend to depend on.

"Tell me something, Lori. If you don't have faith in his confidence, why are you his friend?"

"There's something just a little bit bad about him. I've always had a weakness for the criminal element."

"Hold up! Kent is a criminal?"

"Caroline Grant, give me a break. He has an edge that appeals to me. But he's just not *bad* enough to make me shout to the gods."

"The last thing I want in a man is 'bad.'"

"To each her own."

Caroline shook her head, at a loss to understand Lori. "What's 'bad' got to do with confidence?" she asked.

For the longest time she got no reply. Caroline knew she'd acted like that hero in Texas history, William Barret Travis, by drawing a line in the sand. She didn't feel much remorse over it. Getting to the gist of Kent Mackay was important. Friendship wasn't on the line here. It was love.

"Lori Hardwicke, talk. Now."

"Once I got a line on Kent's insecurities, I checked further into his background. You know, into his childhood. He was a scrappy kid, to give him credit. Ignoring the childhood bullies who made fun of his scar. Finding a way to get past a speech impediment. Working two jobs while he went to college on a scholarship. And never a soul to help him along. That's the stuff of a survivor."

On occasion Caroline had tried to picture Kent's youth, but it was never so vivid as now. She glanced down the office and out the floor-to-ceiling window, where cars dotted the parking lot, an assortment of people walking to wherever their destinies took them.

Dear Kent, he had forged his own destiny. He'd done as she'd tried to. Gone somewhere.

"I've never known a more confident man, but he's human," she said, feeling each of her failures and admiring his many successes. "There's a soft core that haunts him."

"It does more than haunt, Caroline. It consumes him."

I know. "Why is he troubled? He's got everything going for him."

"He can't leave his childhood behind, or forget his origins. Despite his successes, he's still a little boy, his nose pressed against the candy-store window, wishing he could know the sweet succor of decent parents."

"What does Kent know about his parents?"

Rising from the sofa, Lawyer Lady picked up her purse. "Gracious. Look how late it's gotten. I'm late for my appointment at the hairdresser's. Later, 'gator."

"If you think I'll let you tease me like that, then hare off to the beauty shop, you are sadly mistaken. Sit down. I want to know all about Kent's parents."

"Ask Kent."

"I can't. We had a…a disagreement before he left for Houston. Lori, this is important. I love Kent, but not knowing his head is like a lawyer asking a question without having the answer in advance. Help me."

Lori wavered, glanced downward, then at Caroline. "I had a case of Scotch imported. It's in the car. Why don't I get a bottle? You find some glasses?"

Caroline had the time. Angie was taking Natalie home with her tonight, to get the child's mind off missing Kent. "We shouldn't drink and drive."

"If you don't have cab fare, I'll loan it to you."
"Get the Scotch."

It had been a long week. The longest of Kent Mackay's life. He'd dealt with the Fourth Estate and had done as best he could with the chairman of Lisle Shipping Line, a huge project, considering the man's God complex.

During it all, Kent suffered. Wanting to call Caroline, needing to, but her well-being took precedence. She'd be better off, getting on with the getting on.

He didn't expect her to be at the penthouse. The sun had set as he entered the building that housed his home. His home? It had been their home.

His suit coat moored to his shoulder by a finger, a new hanging bag in his other hand, he spoke to Cherin, entered the elevator and turned the key that engaged the mechanism. He could be resolute from here to eternity, but Kent knew it wouldn't be easy to step into a shell of a house. That was what it would be. A shell. Without Caroline, and Gnat Nat, there would be no life to the quarters.

When he entered the great room, he lost his grip on the coat as well as his hanging bag. She sat on the sofa, staring into the cold fireplace.

"You're home." Why hadn't he said something profound? He yearned to lop off the distance between them, and tell her how much he'd missed her, then fold her into arms that begged for the feel of her.

One feminine hand made a fist in her lap, the other curling around the sash of her bathrobe. She turned to him, her expression even colder than a dead fire. "Tell me about yourself."

Without a doubt, she knew the truth. How? From

Lori? From Ted O'Banyon? It had to be Lori. How much could she tell, though? And hadn't she ever heard of loyalty? He tamped irritation, accepting that it was natural for girlfriends to confide.

"It's nice to see you, too, Caro." What luck, his earnings ability was not dependent on his skills as a communicative lover. Maybe he'd never become loquacious of speech. Maybe he just ought to accept that.

"I'll check on Gnat Nat."

"She's missed you."

His gait hurried, he went to the room he and Caroline had outfitted in the cutest of accoutrements. In bed, with teddy bears and a purple dinosaur as companions, Natalie slept in a ball. He ran the edge of a forefinger along her cheek.

It roused her; fringed eyes opened. "Kenn. 'Uv you."

"I love you, too, Gnat Nat."

"S'eepy." She curled fingers around his forefinger, hanging on as if he were a lifeline. Her eyes closed. "Mommy mad. Mommy cry."

Mommy? That part was good. "I'll make her stop crying," he promised, yet wondered if such was possible. And if he should try to piece together their dichotomy, even if he could.

Once he knew Natalie was asleep again, he left her room.

He half expected Caroline to be in her own room, but she remained as he'd left her. "Mind if I sit down?"

"Go right ahead. It's your home. But I expect to hear the truth from you. Home is where the heart is, to use a tired-out phrase." She gestured toward her chest. "This is my heart. It's here. Now. And it hurts."

He loosened his tie and the top button of his shirt, hoping to get much needed air into his lungs. "I don't want to hurt you. Never wanted to."

"You just can't face up to your beginnings, can you? You went to Ted O'Banyon and got a report on your parents. But you couldn't even share the results with your best friend, much less with me. Is it so bad, whatever it is with your mother and father?"

"Yes, it is." No unfastened button could give enough air.

"I can't imagine anything bad enough to keep us apart."

He didn't want to lie to Caroline. To do so would be the ultimate insult. But he had to. "Like I told you in Chez Goyette, I'm not interested in marriage."

"You asked some redheaded twit to be your wife. You didn't love her. You love me. Why the difference, Kent?"

"I love you too much." He didn't dare look at her.

"You have a strange way of showing it."

He needed space. "Good night, Caro."

He got the hell away by stomping to his bedroom. There, he yanked off his shirt and snaked the belt from trouser loops. Somehow he shucked the rest of his clothes and whipped back bed linens. Too bad he couldn't take much comfort from laying his head on his own pillow for the first time in days.

Caroline opened his door, light from the hall behind her, showing off her voluptuous form to its best advantage. Dammit.

"I forgive you," she announced.

He didn't want forgiveness. He didn't know what

he wanted, but the reasonable part of his brain warned not to go with his desires. His passion. His need that was every bit as voluptuous as Caroline's body.

Her body. A palsy went through him as she neared his bed. He almost wheezed as she drew that robe from her shoulders; he forgot to breathe when material pooled at her feet. She stood nude before him, breasts heavy, waist trim, hips flared.

Like the jack-in-the-box in a nearby room, his arousal jumped up, elevating the top sheet. Kent turned to his side. "I've got a headache, Caro."

"Do you now?" She eased to the bed.

Perfume, her usual perfume, tickled his nostrils. Her fingers, magical fingers, traced his arm and circled his elbow. Somewhat in the neighborhood of forty thousand impulses went through him, each of them centering on his groin that wrestled with sensitivity, understanding and any thought of what a loving woman expected out of her nineties man. He wanted to do as men had done since they had first crawled from beneath rocks. Kent wanted to make love to Caroline so hard and fast that their heads would spin and their bodies would soar.

What a cool thing to consider, the voice of reason said. It was the same voice that had gotten him through the trials and tribulations of a wretched existence, and had forced an abandoned boy's feet in the right direction.

He stilled a finger as it delved into his navel. "Stop."

"Lovers should never sleep on an argument."

Her voice, heady and soft, seeped into his veins, getting reason into a headlock. But that voice was a fighter. And it reminded Kent he was in deep.

"Get out of here," he demanded.

But she plucked at the sheet and drew it away from his body. "Nice." She straddled his thigh. "How long do you think you'll last, trying to deny you want what I want? You're about six inches longer than you were when I walked through that door."

"No."

"Okay, seven inches."

"Six. I had an inch or two to begin with."

She laughed, a lusty sound. Her fingers did wicked, appealing things to the member in question. "Nice."

"When I said no—" he grabbed her hand "—I meant stop."

Her tongue flicking his ear. "When? Now?" The tips of her breasts were sliding up and down his flesh. "Or now?"

He set her aside. "No means no."

That stopped her. But it didn't stop her ire. "You...you *lawyer*." Apparently that was the worst insult she could come up with at the spur of the moment. "See if I care!"

She fought tears, he knew. If there was one thing he couldn't stand, it was her tears. Just as she started to marshal dignity and rise from the bed, he rolled her beneath him. Chest met breasts. His knee moved between hers. A seeking hand found her femininity. The sun should never rise on an argument.

But she was an evil, vindictive thing. "I thought you said no meant no."

"I've changed my mind."

Kent pressed forward with every inch to his person, burying himself in Caroline's heat. The caveman met his match.

* * *

One of the least popular things for a man to do, postcoitus *amor,* was to reply to a question, and speak the truth about why he refused to become a father. But Kent was through with subterfuge. ''I refuse to pass bad genes to your children.''

''What drivel.''

He quit the plate of grapes and cheese they were eating in his king-size bed, the tiny lights of airborne planes through the window coloring the darkened sky. ''Caro, you never heard of a bad seed? Having been one, I take exception to 'drivel.' I've spent my adult life not passing my blood to others.''

She stayed put, where they clustered as if this were a narrow cot. ''Let me repeat, what drivel.'' She chewed the last grape. ''You're smart, you're ambitious, you're successful. You could model men's underwear. A face like yours could grace the silver screen. If you've got bad genes, I'm a monkey's uncle.''

How could she say that, when he'd suffered so much rejection? Suffered since the day of his birth, when his father sneered at the birth registrar, and said, ''You choose the brat's given name.'' The new father lit a Kent cigarette, then crushed the pack and lobbed it over his back. Once he'd hustled the empty-armed mother out the door, the official had likened that crumpled cellophane package to a baby abandoned. ''Kent'' got inserted as his given name. It was all in Ted O'Banyon's report.

Kent tapped the control to the bedside lamps, bathing the area in muted light, and said to Caroline, ''You offend me.''

''I don't see how.'' Her thumb jabbed between her

bottom teeth, plucking once. She was being way too calm about this, showing none of her compassion.

He lunged to his feet, stomping over to the window and clamping hands beneath his armpits.

The sun would rise on their argument.

Again, he faced west, taking a deep breath. "Remember that day I 'joked' with you about Don Perry's parents? Do you recall my making light of a mother who runs a house of prostitution? Think about what I said about the man who's in prison for murder."

Understand me, accept me. At least try to understand. Say it's all right, when I tell you. Say it doesn't matter.

Kent whipped around. His gaze welded to Caroline's. "Of course those weren't Don's parents. They're mine."

There was no understanding in Caroline's expression.

Too often Kent had mentally rehearsed this moment and had tried to prepare for it. No way could he have prepared for the loathing in Caroline's face. It was as if she were eyeing an apple with a worm slithering from its fine red skin.

Wasn't she?

Chapter Fourteen

They had come this far for Kent to blather about his *parents?*

A few static moments past his confession about the Mackay pedigree, Caroline grabbed her discarded robe and beat a retreat to her lent bedroom, feeling every bit as confined as Greezy did. If not for disturbing Baby, she would leave this instant, hang the nebulous results of huffing off.

Yet it was useless, erasing the image of an anguished face. Kent's face. So much in her mind's eye.

In the long stretch while awaiting his return from Houston, after she'd gotten good and drunk on Lori's fancy Scotch, she'd been certain he'd have a reasonable explanation. And had held on to hope. Reasons—his didn't make sense. Not before she'd seduced him, nor afterward.

Blather.

He was full of it, and...

Lies.

It was preposterous, Caroline recalling a joke at a moment like this, but she did. How did one spot a lying lawyer? *If he's talking, he's lying.*

He may have lied about the Mackay genealogy—absurd. He could have lied about loving Caroline. Too brutal to think about. How much more could she take of his behavior?

How much more did she wish to take?

"What next, Caro?"

At his voice, she rendered a look of indecision in its direction. Still as nude as when they made hot love, he centered the doorjamb, his features even more troubled. She swam against the wash of sympathy crying out to make things better.

"Who knows what's next?" She shoved arms into her robe. "But your excuse for not committing isn't enough for me."

He squinted upward. "Caro, I won't ever father a child. Fruit doesn't fall far from the tree."

What a joke. Not one word had he listened to, when she'd tried to help him. Yes, what a joke, his refusal. He'd done a very good job of initiating what got a child, as her inner thighs could prove. "Why didn't you say so, that night you acted like a total jerk? Or in the interim?"

"Some things are difficult to discuss."

"How right." She sank to her own bed, the springs protesting. She wouldn't think about springs and what they meant to whatever she had with Kent. She recalled another night, another place, another man, that one clothed. Clothed, and girded with the finest product of the brewer's art. "Frank said those exact words. What a guy."

Her ex had provided an oil-tanker load of condescension and scorn, not to mention his final lie of omission. Once, she read that people tend to be attracted to the same sort of person, no matter how many times they gagged on reality. Once, she'd disagreed. Once.

"Why don't you get yourself a beer, down it, then let loose with a big, barking belch? I'd feel right at home."

Kent stepped forward, stopping in front of her. It wasn't brew she smelled. Sandalwood, man, a whiff of sex—these almost got to her, almost made her forget. Almost.

"I'm not Frank," he said. "I'm Kent."

"Goodbye, Kent."

He sat down heavily, beside her. Like he'd done the night of his temper tantrum, he clutched the edges as if holding on for dear life. "I don't want to say goodbye."

"I'm taking Baby. As for your consolation prize of Easy Access, the keys are in my purse. I'll leave them on a table."

"Don't do this, Caro. It's taxing enough already."

"I've taken enough of your charity. Be on notice. I've resigned from Easy Access."

"You need that job, Caro. Without it, you'll be out of work, basically out of money. You have nothing tangible to take to court. You won't last five minutes in front of Judge Miller. He might think you're out for Gnat Nat's money."

Before, she'd hurt, was indignant. Now he did the same thing Frank was a master at. Belittlement. Frank laughed at her ambitions, disregarded her dreams. Kent decried her abilities. This man hurt her as the past one never could.

"And you're not out for money, Mr. Four Hundred An Hour?"

"I've never billed one dime to Natalie's account."

"If you're not bilking Baby, then you're draining poor schleps like Snappy Sours."

"This is a first. Hearing big business called a schlep."

"There's a first for everything." She shot from bed and trod the floor, like the restless cat that she was. "Let's hope you're upright enough to stand back and let me take Baby from here. She doesn't need you." *That's a lie. Baby loves him, cries for him.* So did Caroline. They would get over Kent, somehow. Someday. Maybe.

"Caro, I don't intend to let you go. I love that kid. I love you." He was standing now, trying to bring her to his chest. "Is it possible you can forgive me, accept me, give me another chance? Knowing there'll be no children between us?"

A repeat of history.

She backed away, until her hips hit the dresser. "You think this is over *kids?*"

"Isn't it?"

Was it? Yes. His attitude about fatherhood attacked her weakest place. Her pride.

It did nothing to ease her pain, his saying, "Can't you understand? I'm a product of inferior parents."

"Aren't we both?"

"My mother...she has to make a living. It's not her I resent as much as I do my old man. He was always a felon, just one step ahead of the police. Fifteen years ago the law caught up with him. He's serving a life sentence, no chance for parole. For stabbing that exotic dancer. Over a hundred times with a screwdriver."

"Oh, Kent, no." Caroline's heart went out to the brutal mementoes that followed in his shadow. It was now understandable, his aversion to screwdrivers.

"I don't judge people by their pedigree. How could I?" she reasoned. "Remember my mother? Enough said. I wonder about Baby's maternal gene pool. Well, what's the use debating that?"

She waited for correlations to dawn, but they didn't. He explained, "My father never got his cleft palate corrected."

That. So it was an inherited feature. One within the realm of correction. "You just don't get it, do you, Kent? It wouldn't have mattered if your parents were apes at the zoo, or if you'd been some sort of botched conception experiment in a laboratory. It wouldn't have mattered if you'd been uglier than a goat. I fell for the man inside you. But you're not that man. I'm revolted by the *you* beneath your mustache."

He flinched.

She ached to embrace him, and apologize for her hurtful words, but wouldn't. She gathered her clothes and put them on.

"You didn't seem to mind my mustache when we were making love," he argued.

"If you're looking for a compliment, keep trying," she shot back, her recalcitrant body remembering exactly how that mustache had felt.

He spoke a non sequitur. "What about adopting kids?"

"Hold up, Mackay. You never even asked to marry me, yet you ask such a question."

"What about adopted ones?"

"Since I'll soon be in the throes of adopting a child, I think the answer to that is a given."

"We could get married. Add to the family through adoption. What about it, Caro?"

She refused to reply. Not once did she glance at Kent while belongings got dragged out of the closet and dresser. Shoving the mass into her father's old suitcase, she clamped her fingers around the handle and huffed past Kent.

He caught her arm. "Marry me, Caro."

Piecing together a broken man just wasn't within her powers. Maybe it had to do with her own heritage. No. More like environment. How could she cure him, when she'd never been thoroughly healed?

"I won't have a man who won't father my children."

The next Friday, Ted O'Banyon lumbered into Kent's office and tossed a report to the desk. "Read it and weep," said the husky investigator. "It's all there."

A neatly typed label gave the subject: Caroline Grant.

"Good show, O'Banyon. Close the door on your way out."

At first Kent couldn't open the folder. Maybe he'd never open it. He eyed File Thirteen.

He brushed fingers across his lips and leaned back in the executive chair, closing his eyes. Lost. He'd never been this empty of zeal, even when he'd been tossed between foster homes and institutions for unwanted children.

He'd taken a gamble with Caroline and lost.

That was the part he couldn't get over.

Her rejection.

He'd never let himself care too much for another woman. Never, ever. But why wouldn't the ache go away? *Because I love her. Because I'll never quit loving her.* There would never be any other woman for Kent Mackay.

A given.

He was miserable.

He even missed that damned old cat.

It had been this way, in the aftermath of her departure. He couldn't stand to be at home. Everywhere he turned, there was a reminder of Caroline. Already he'd called a real-estate agent and had put his bachelor pad on the market.

Would he never again see the woman he loved? Of course he would. They were linked. Natalie would have their combined attentions for the next sixteen years, plus.

He opened the file. Caroline had rented a small house in a respectable neighborhood, had paid deposits for utilities. As he'd known, she hadn't gone near Easy Access.

Lori Hardwicke chose that moment to bounce into his office, slamming the door behind her, the sound no doubt reverberating to the secretarial suite. Hands on her hips, she advanced on him.

"Back on the toast and chopped nails diet, Lori?"

"Give me that file. Now."

"What file?" There were hundreds of open cases within the firm, yet he had his suspicions. "What are you talking about?"

"Caroline's file, nincompoop. Ted told me—you had him beating the streets, looking for her."

"O'Banyon betrayed me?"

"No. I found out on my own. And I won't let you invade Caroline's space."

Kent crossed arms over his chest, rearing for a fight. "Where's your loyalty?"

"With my client. Don't look so shocked. Are you surprised Caroline wants me as attorney? I'll be in court with her. I plan to petition to take the Perry trusteeship away from you."

Just when he thought he couldn't hurt any more, this! "Get serious, Lori. You have no grounds, and you know it. Stick to your specialty. Leave Don Perry's last wishes to me."

She leaned over to flatten her palms on his desk, her blue eyes the iciest he'd ever seen. "You've done enough damage, counselor. You botched your chances with Ruth Perry's daughters. Just like you did with that redhead."

"I don't need this. I can't deal with it. If you want the truth, I don't give a damn about redheads. That's past history. But I do care about Caroline. And Gnat Nat. I'm the best party to oversee the trust. Caro is done with me, but I will, as long as there's a breath in my body, make certain the Perry sisters have the kind of representation no amount of money can buy. The best. The kind that has love behind it."

"You're too close to the situation. That makes for bad lawyering, and you know it."

"Inform your so-called client you won't appear in court with her. She has representation already. And that's final."

"She'll fight you on this."

He groaned, recalling how he'd hurt Caroline's pride. Bad move, undercutting her abilities. But he'd done it in desperation. Blood did tell.

Should he give in? It would return that which he'd stolen: her pride.

"Kent, why won't you fight for her?"

His eyes burned. Something happened, something that hadn't occurred since his childhood. A tear ran down his cheek. "Lori, I don't know how to fight for her."

Kent Mackay fought dirty.

Not only was Caroline brokenhearted, she had to suffer the indignity of a threatened lawsuit. That rotten scoundrel had papers served on "the defendant," at her rented, compact home. Abide by the terms of her oral agreement to remain as Director of Easy Access, a "nonprofit organization chartered by the State of Texas," or face the complainant in District Court.

She returned to Easy Access.

Kent dropped the suit. And he didn't once show his face at her place of employment. One would think—and Caroline had—he'd stop by to check on his investment.

He was lost to her. Forever and always.

She tried not to think about Kent—an impossibility, since she cried each night away. But she did concentrate her daytime efforts on being a single mom and giving hope and help to those in need.

As the date set for the court hearing on the adoption and trusteeship neared, she found herself somewhat glad Lori would represent the family concerns. She had one friend, in and out of court.

Was there anything else to take comfort from? Caroline need not face Kent in a court of law.

Chapter Fifteen

October fifteenth. The big day had arrived. This morning, the Honorable Brian Miller of the Probate Court, Dallas District, would sit in judgment in the Matter of Natalie Suzanne Perry, Minor. The sky was black.

And where might Lorraine Hardwicke be found?

She'd promised to rendezvous at the parking lot nearest Dallas's infamous grassy knoll. "She's late," her client groused to herself.

At the point she could wait no longer, Caroline set a course for the Records Building, ignoring traffic, pedestrians and the threat of weather.

People stood at the base of the steps leading to the main floor of the half-modern, half-aged courthouse, but not a one of those individuals was Lori.

Caroline worried the tight bun at her nape, the kind fashioned to make an impression in court. What was keeping Lori? And had she kept her promise about holding the media at bay? It was important that no sensational headlines follow Natalie's adoption. Lori had assured her, "It cost me the rest of my precious case of MacAllan Scotch, but a friend of mine will divert reporters to a wild-goose chase."

That had been yesterday.

Today, what?

Settle down. You have no reason to doubt Lori.

What would she have done without Lori here lately? However, she could have done without the constant advice, "Kent needs to be needed." Caroline had done everything she could think of to make him feel needed. What more could she do?

The reasonable thing was to go on to Probate Court Number One. Lori would be there, without a doubt.

Soon, Caroline was on the main floor, passing through the metal detector. A crowd banked the elevators. Some were obviously seeking to untangle the legal webs that might entrap them. Some looked like lawyers. Lori wasn't among them. But...wasn't that? Surely not? Well, why not? Kent Mackay was an attorney. It stood to reason he might be here.

Too unstrung to confront the man she would always love, Caroline searched for an alternative to getting trapped in an elevator with him. She spied a placard marked Stairway. Once in the stairwell, she shivered.

A figure suddenly appeared at the top of the stairs. An all-too-familiar man with wide shoulders, with hair as dark as the deepest recesses of this stairwell. Kent.

Caroline steeled herself. Yet she gawked at his shadowed features. And her heart beat wildly.

"Is this...on purpose?" she managed to ask, fearing trickery was afoot, as she climbed the stairs. "What are you doing here?"

"Change of plans. Lori had to go out of town this morning. Business. A state representative got caught, his pants around his ankles, with a junior-high girl in Austin."

"Nice of Lori to let me know."

"I'm letting you know."

"What else do I need to know?" Caroline asked and dreaded the answer.

"I'm going to be in court with you today. I'll see that Lori is made Trustee. I am your friend, Caro." He offered his hand, as if to help her up the final steps to the landing.

If she touched him, Caroline feared she'd back him into the corner, rip his clothes off and make a number of demands. "If you mean to befriend me, do it in front of the judge. Get me my baby. Forever."

"Follow me."

He led her into a tall, well-lit chamber of white marble and carved wood. It was as if she'd stepped into Perry Mason's courtroom, an arena where a round-eyed attorney would expose as unfit a quaking woman in a bargain-basement suit.

She eyed a court reporter and a bailiff, and a handful of spectators, each of the latter having the look of ordinary people interested in eavesdropping on other people's trouble.

Kent motioned to a table that faced the judge's bench. Caroline sat; so did he. He unlatched his attaché case to pull papers from them. A clap of thunder sounded from outside, like a sonic boom. Lightning zigged. The sounds almost cloaked the expletive that the attorney muttered.

"Kent, what's wrong?"

"Perfidy." Storm clouds darkened the sky as well

as the courtroom, but they weren't as black as Kent's face. "The trusteeship papers aren't here."

Panicked, Caroline asked, "Does this mean the adoption won't go through?"

"I said the trusteeship papers. Not the adoption decree. Don't worry."

How could she not, with his reading whatever was in that briefcase, his brow lowered, his mouth set, as if he were poring over execution orders?

"All rise."

There were no Perry Masons in Probate Court Number One. A clerk read aloud, "Case number four-seven-two-eight-three."

Natalie was just another number on the docket? Outside, rain poured. It was as turbulent as Caroline's pulse. Kent Mackay stood to speak before His Honor, in the adoption cause, making a number come alive.

The judge nodded at each of his utterances. Then Brian Miller cast a stern glance over the top of his half glasses. "Are you Caroline Danson Grant?"

"Yes, sir. I am."

"Adopting a child shouldn't be undertaken in haste." Another clap of thunder. "Do you realize what you're asking for?"

"Yes, Your Honor."

He posed more questions before banging his gavel, the sound thundering in Caroline's ears. "Petition granted."

"Gnat Nat is yours," Kent whispered.

Caroline let out a pent-up breath. "By the grace of God and Kent Mackay."

"Counselor, what about the rest of it?"

Kent rubbed his neck and eyed the judge. "May I petition to postpone the trusteeship until a later date?

I'm withdrawing my petition in favor of Lorraine Hardwicke.''

He needs to be needed.

"Judge, can we talk?"

"Sit down, Caro. It's my job to ask to approach the bench. You have no business there."

"Not my business? This is my life! Judge, we have to talk."

"This is irregular." The judge picked up a fountain pen and tapped it twice. "But you may approach, Ms. Grant."

"Caro, no."

"Madame Court Reporter, move closer." A robed arm waved. "We'll need this on record."

Caroline rounded the table and marched up to the judge. Thank heavens Kent was behind her. She wanted him to hear every word. Determined that her voice not carry to the spectators, she spoke lowly and plainly. "Mr. Mackay doesn't think he ought to be Natalie's trustee. But—"

"Caro, sit down!"

The judge banged his gavel. "Order. I've given the lady permission to speak. I will hear what she has to say. Mackay, you may talk later."

Kent shot her a murderous glare, but she ignored it.

"Your Honor, this man, my attorney, lied to me."

She heard a groan, and knew it came from Kent.

Someone from the back of the courtroom moved forward, extending a microrecorder. Great. A reporter. Lori's influence hadn't been strong enough.

After another boom of thunder, Caroline lowered her voice further. "Mr. Mackay said—"

A cellular telephone rang, cutting her off.

"Turn that thing off!" the judge demanded, but the reporter didn't pay heed.

"You're kidding. SWAT has Romeo Swain cornered at Between the Covers bookstore? Yeah, I'll be right there." The reporter jumped two rows of chairs to beat for sensationalism.

At least Lori hadn't let her down about the goose chase. Fred Penny, better known as Romeo Swain, had graced the covers of numerous romance novels. He always drew a crowd. Caroline couldn't imagine how the authorities were going to handle Lori's conspiracy, but that wasn't important at the moment.

Caroline was relieved at the relative privacy.

"Go on, Ms. Grant."

"Mr. Mackay says he doesn't want to be Trustee, but that's a lie. He loves my baby. She loves him. He's the best person for the job, and he knows it. He'd never pilfer her money. Of course, Ms. Hardwicke wouldn't, either, but I want Kent Mackay. Oh, boy, do I want him."

The judge frowned. "Ms. Grant, this isn't the proper place to debate personal problems."

How true. "Since he's been avoiding me, I have to talk here. I owe Mr. Mackay an apology. You see, I let my pride mess up a wonderful relationship. Never has anyone shown me as many kindnesses, nor as much love, as Mr. Mackay did. He was always reasonable and logical, like about Fill-Er-Fast, and he was right about my chances here in this court. Yet I was unkind to him, not sympathizing over his...problems. I long to bear his children, but giving birth is simply another measure of my bloated pride. It's a Ruth thing. The important part is rearing children, not whether they're got the fun way."

"Ms. Grant," the judge began.

"I'll get her out of here." Kent took her elbow.

She jerked from his clutch. "Our future is at stake. The only way you'll make me leave is in handcuffs."

Two groans this time, one each from Kent and the judge.

"I don't know the law, nor do I understand genetics," she said. "I do know my heart. I love this man. I *need* him. Not just for Natalie, although she needs him every day, every hour."

Amusement crossed the judge's face. "Irrelevant, but interesting."

Caroline boosted her nose. "We're a motley threesome—me, Kent and Baby. None of us comes from a world-class gene pool, but I think we've done all right for ourselves."

"Gotta muzzle her," Kent muttered.

"Baby felt secure for a while there, when Mr. Mackay was a father figure to her. She could grow up just fine, with him around. I've done pretty good for a motherless kid. I educated myself, and I found a darn—oops, I guess I shouldn't say darn. Anyhow, I have a career that benefits the unfortunates of this society, and I have Mr. Mackay to thank for that. If you know him personally, you're aware of his many strides in life."

"Your Honor, I *will* settle this matter in private." Once more Kent took her arm; this time there was no getting free, his grip being as ironlike as manacles.

"Good luck, Mackay." The judge leaned back in his chair and chuckled. "This could be the day you'll lose for the first time."

"Losers can be winners," Caroline added.

Kent wasn't listening. The furious attorney hustled her out of the courtroom and into that stairway landing, the very spot where she'd been tempted to corner him.

* * *

Kent had her cornered. Which was a better place than letting Caroline run loose, for certain. "You're a brazen thing."

"So?"

"I'll be a laughingstock in Miller's eyes from now on."

"Better you should care about what I think."

His gaze went upward, past the single bulb that lighted the stairwell. "God in heaven, what goes with this woman?"

"I love you. And I mean to be yours. Forever."

Kent went still. A half second later he planted his palm above her shoulder, leaning toward her. Her perfume—pure Caroline mingled with flowery oils—drifted to his nostrils and spread through veins too long denied a sensory delight. The cat eyes that had enticed him from day one, now swept upward, luring, beguiling.

"Why don't you tell me...?" His finger traced her jaw. "I'd like to hear everything you intended to say in court."

"I want you—I need you!—forever and ever. No matter what it takes to get you."

"You would've said that in court? Don't answer. Obviously you would have."

"Why not? I love you." She tapped his chest. "You love me, too. Right here in the middle of your heart. You lied, of course. Could be you don't know your mind. It's screwed up. You don't think you're worthy of love. Or of taking chances. For a smart man, you sure are dumb."

She spoke the truth. For all his successes Kent was still a kid struggling. Funny, though. Those weeks in the duplex, Caroline had taken the kid out of him.

"Baby and I need you," she said. "Just like I needed Easy Access, you need us."

"I—I can't argue that."

"The three of us are pretty darn special. Genes or no genes." Caroline eyed him squarely. "Think about that."

He had been thinking about it. Ever since he'd opened his briefcase and had found a report from a geneticist instead of those trusteeship papers. The switch, a certain law partner's doing, he had no doubt. Chances were, he and Caro could produce a child with problems, but the rest of society took chances, too.

"Neither one of us deals from a strong deck, Kent, but I've seen enough of this world, and read enough about its people, to know something. Even the best bluestocking can make a kid who looks like Quasimodo or becomes a lowlife. Some of this earth's finest heroes and heroines hailed from parents worse than ours. We'd have a fifty-fifty chance of getting an Einstein. Adoption is the same that way. A crap shoot."

"Adoption? I was talking about..." He laughed. "Caro, we'd be taking a chance either way."

"We could stop at the one child we have. I'm willing."

How had he ever gotten so lucky? If one of the other Hardwicke attorneys had represented Perry, if the donor egg hadn't taken, if the Perrys had lived, if Caroline had still been married to Frank Grant—that made Kent gulp.

His fingers found the curve of her hip. "What would you think about my taking a chance? You know what I mean."

Lashes fluttered as she made him suffer. "You want to grow hothouse orchids?"

"Lori and her big mouth." Fingers eased into Caroline's hair, dislodging the bun. "What do you think about growing...fruit."

"Kumquats?"

"Quit." Chuckling, he tugged on her ear. "There's a place around the corner where we could get blood tests. I have some pull with the management. We could be back here in an hour to ask for a marriage license. Miller can marry us."

"Excellent idea. But what about the 'fruit'?"

"Let's leave the planting till afterward."

The lone light above had never shone with as much wattage as when it reflected in Caroline's eyes. The sun didn't shine this brightly. She pressed her lips to Kent's. The earth moved. No, it was the building, shaken by thunder, but who cared?

"You're full of excellent ideas, Mackay."

Epilogue

This, in a way, was their first anniversary. One year ago today, Kent had served as stork, arriving at Caroline's duplex with Natalie. The stork had made a couple more visits to the Mackay's University Park home, one visit a month after he and Caroline were married and two weeks after Judge Miller had changed Natalie's last name to theirs.

"Last July, who would've ever thought," Kent said to his wife, as she patted their baby son's back and they waited on the family room sofa for "Aunt" Lori to return their two older children from an outing to the Marsalis Zoo, "we'd end up a quintet. And so soon."

Danny burped.

"All I can say is, it's a good thing I got to you in a court of law, Mackay."

"True."

The pills hadn't worked. By the time they said "I do," young Danson Mackay was already on the way. While they might have picked his grandfather's full name for Danny, they couldn't. Their chosen son, now pushing four, already had the name George. Jorge, really, but it translated to George. They had learned about him at Easy Access; both Kent and Caroline fell in love with the boy at first sight.

"Hey, chick. Want to try for a sextet?"

"Do you want me to hit you with this teddy bear?" Caroline, laughing, stuck out her tongue. "Nothing else is ever going in that can inflate to eleven pounds."

"What about last night?" Kent wiggled brows.

"Oooh, that is low of you, reminding me of my base instincts," she teased in return.

"I intend to keep reminding you."

She tweaked Kent's mustache. "You do fight dirty."

Danny complained.

"Let me hold him." Kent held out his arms and wiggled each finger in turn. "Come to Papa."

"Fine. I need to install that Johnny jump-up thing, anyhow." Caroline, kissing the top of Danny's head, handed over thirteen pounds of boy, then began to exit the family room.

Kent might have offered to turn a few screws with the baby contraption. He'd gotten pretty good at being a handyman. But he was not going to pass up an opportunity for father-son bonding.

His heart swelling and his chest puffing, he gazed down at the most beautiful baby, and third most-beautiful child, in the world. "Say, fella, how you doing today? Mommy been good to you? Feeding you all right?"

Danny spat up.

"George and I are going to make a ballplayer out of you. You keep on eating. We want you big and strong."

While Kent wiped up Danny's response, he heard noises from the foyer. Apparently Natalie and George were home. About two seconds later, the Tornadoes found him and Danny.

Kent made room in his arms for two more perfect children. He loved each of his children in different, yet equal, ways. Natalie was Daddy's girl. With George, he felt a special affinity. It was just as easy to love Danny.

"You know, kiddos, your daddy is a lucky, lucky man."

"He's at it again."

"I know, Lori. I know."

The ladies watched from the next room as Kent clutched all three children. But the older ones soon tired of cuddling, Natalie running to her playhouse and George limping behind her.

"One more surgery, and George'll walk without braces." Caroline stepped back. "He wants to play ball, like other kids."

"It's a good thing, what you've done." Lori picked up Greezy to scratch between whiskers. "I guess it's Kent's way of treating an afflicted child as he wanted to be treated."

"It's more the chemistry of love. Kent was ready to accept a child, no matter the imperfections. George just showed up earlier than Danny." It was probably postpartum blues, but Caroline couldn't help quivering her chin. How could she love a child so much, yet...
"I'm awful. After all my big talk about accepting things as they are, I just look at Danny, and bawl."

"Caro, he's not that bad."

"Danny could grow up to be the fat man of the circus."

"Don't be ridiculous. He'll trim down. Hopefully."

Caroline walked back to the family room. There Kent was, smiling rapturously at his son. She smiled, too. The blues left as she studied the two males. So what if Danny was so fat that his eyes were lost in the puffs of his face? Surely he'd grow hair above his ears, and those inch-long, spiky black bristles growing on the top of his head would flatten down.

Kent caught sight of her. "Come here and kiss your gorgeous son."

She did, the chemistry of love flowing freely.

Danny might have a face that only this father could love, but his mother adored him, too. While Kent didn't seem to notice that the puffs deflated as time passed, Caroline did. And she heaved a major sigh of relief when it turned out that Danny was not going to have a bad-hair life.

* * * * *

Silhouette
SPECIAL EDITION
™

That's My Baby!

April 1997 WHAT TO DO ABOUT BABY
by Martha Hix (SE #1093)
When a handsome lawyer showed up on Carolyn Grant's
doorstep with a toddler in tow, she didn't know what to think.
Suddenly, she had a little sister she'd never known about...and
a *very* persistent man intent on making Caro his own....

June 1997 HIS DAUGHTER'S LAUGHTER
by Janis Reams Hudson (SE #1105)
Carly Baker came to widower Tyler Barnett's ranch to help
his fragile daughter—and connected emotionally with the
caring father and tenderhearted girl. But when Tyler's
interfering in-laws began stirring up trouble, would Carly be
forced to give up the man and child she loved?

And in August, be sure to check out...

ALISSA'S MIRACLE
by
Ginna Gray (SE#1117)

He'd told her that he could never have a child, and lovely
widow Alissa Kirkpatrick was so in love with enigmatic
Dirk Matheson that she agreed to a childless marriage. Until
the pregnancy test proved positive....

THAT'S MY BABY!
**Sometimes, bringing up baby can bring
surprises...and showers of love.**

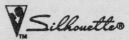

In April 1997
Bestselling Author

DALLAS SCHULZE

takes her Family Circle series to new heights with

TESSA'S CHILD

In April 1997 Dallas Schulze brings readers a
brand-new, longer, out-of-series title featuring the
characters from her popular Family Circle miniseries.

When rancher Keefe Walker found Tessa Wyndham he
knew that she needed a man's protection—she was
pregnant, alone and on the run from a heartless past.
Keefe was also hiding from a dark past...but in one
overwhelming moment he and Tessa forged a family
bond that could never be broken.

Available in April wherever books are sold.